★ ★ ★

A Journey Worth Taking

SYDNEY & WILL

A Journey Series Novella

A Journey Worth Taking
Copyright © 2023 by Alexandra Grace

All rights reserved.

No part of this book may be reproduced or transmitted in any form or by any means, electronic or mechanical, including photocopying and recording, or by any information storage or retrieval system, without permission in writing from the author.

This is a work of fiction. Names, characters, businesses, events, and incidents described in this publication, except for those known in the public domain, are the products of the author's imagination. Any resemblance to actual persons, living or dead, or actual locales or events is entirely coincidental.

Cover design by GetCovers

Follow me on Instagram and Facebook: @authoralexandragrace

Website: https://authoralexandragrace.carrd.co

The Journey Series
by Alexandra Grace

The Journey Series is best enjoyed in the below order.

(Prequel Novella)
A JOURNEY WORTH TAKING

(Jackson's Story)
A JOURNEY SPARED

A JOURNEY TO LOVE

A JOURNEY HOME

(Sydney's Story)
A JOURNEY BEYOND

To first loves.

Prologue

Sydney's Journal

December 20th

Something's wrong. I can feel it. There's a sharp pain in my gut like a gunshot wound, and my ability to stay strong and positive is seeping out through the entry point.

It's 2 AM. I haven't been able to sleep, eat, or relax for hours. When I opened my journal, the goal was to write out my feelings, hoping to make it all stop. Conjure up an explanation to talk me off the ledge. But here I am…teetering on the edge about to jump.

I can't stop begging the universe to send me a sign and pull me back to safety. Something that says he's safe. Something that proves my instincts wrong and rationalizes what I'm experiencing. But nothing's come, and the bullet continues to grind through my insides.

Visions of him lying in a ditch, bleeding, and helpless in a foreign country have begun to torture me. Doesn't help that I can feel him. Feel his pain and fear as though we're together. I'd give anything to make that happen. Even if it meant taking a bullet to the stomach again. Anything to hear his voice and the sweet words of affirmation that roll so poetically off his tongue. Anything to see his deep brown eyes and feel his tender touch on my skin.

Why couldn't we have met before he signed up for another tour? Why hadn't our paths crossed at a time that would have allowed us to be together longer? Forever is what I want. But who knows when I'll get him back. IF I'll get him back.

Please, God, bring him home to me.

Chapter One

✯ ✯ ✯

Eight Months Earlier

Sydney

"Bye, Nora!" I yell to my roommate, propping the front door open with my foot while juggling an armload of books. "I'm meeting my new boyfriend at the library!"

Biting the inside of my cheek, I silently start the countdown for her appearance and the questions that will follow. Three, two—

"Wait," she calls and jogs into the tiny living room as predicted. "What boyfriend? When did you lower the back-off flag long enough to meet someone? And why wasn't your best friend there with you?"

I lift the books a smidge, giving her a clue.

"Oh. Got it," she says slowly and stares at me with wide I-forgot-you-were-crazy eyes. "Book boyfriend. So not the same."

"Nope. Better."

She shakes her head, surely wondering if I will ever snap out of my dating ban. But it was initiated for a reason, and she knows better than anyone why I enforce it with no exceptions.

"Anyway," she begins, dismissing my comment. "We're meeting at Malone's tonight, right?"

"Yes. Seven o'clock. Text Carlie to remind her, will ya? You know she'll be late if we don't."

"Sure. Do you need help?" She takes in the stack of books.

"Nah. It's just a few books."

"No. It's more like a tower of books. What do you need all those for anyway?"

Lifting my leg, I rest the heavy load on my knee to give my arms a break. "I have an Econ project due soon, and I may have grabbed a few romance novels the last time I was there."

"Whatever. Just don't drop those *boyfriends* or you'll be marrying them."

With a wink, I back out, letting the door slam shut behind me. Nora isn't a reader. She doesn't understand how one book is rarely enough to get me through the week. Excluding mid-term or final weeks, I usually read a book every two days. It's what keeps me grounded and my thoughts off my recent breakup with Trevor (A.K.A. The Reason I Only Date Fictional Men Now).

Good men, I've concluded, are only found in romance novels. Give me a romantic book boyfriend over any in the flesh.

Climbing down the two flights of stairs, I only juggle the book tower twice—first, when Ms. Stanley's four-legged reason for everything ran between my feet at the turn between floors, and second when all three hundred pounds of Ms. Stanley huffed by in a tizzy on the last step.

Ms. Stanley's prize chihuahua escapes almost daily, and she's never less than frazzled over it. Doesn't matter that he has yet to leave the grassy area between our complex and the next. He gets too distracted by the bushes and mulch along the brick to get into any real trouble. But by Ms. Stanley's reaction, you'd think he zipped through multiple lanes of a crowded freeway with every getaway.

"Good luck, Ms. Stanley," I call when she huffs by.

Upon reaching the sidewalk, I start my hike to the public library three blocks away. By block two, I'm wondering why in the world I didn't borrow Nora's car. I could have taken my own if it would start. A mechanic or anything remotely resembling a mechanic, I am not. Don't even know how to check the pressure in my tires or when to change the oil.

I'm a disgrace to independent women everywhere. Especially since I might have to suck up my pride and ask a man to fix it. I could ask the guy who brings his motorcycle helmet into class for help. He looks like he could figure out what's wrong with it.

Ugh. But he'll probably want something in return, and that's the last thing I need. He's made no effort to hide his interest when I catch him eyeing me from across the classroom.

Walking isn't so bad. But men are.

This would be a whole lot easier if my puny arm muscles had more endurance. Maybe I'll add in a round of push-ups during future reading marathons.

Stopping at the next traffic light, I adjust the load to my left hip and shake out my right arm since it now feels like cooked spaghetti. Then, feeling reenergized, I repeat the feat on the other side.

Who needs a car?

When the light changes, I cross the street with a new pep in my step. At this rate, I'll have time to return the books and peruse the romance section before my shift. But in taking the turn at the bank where I work, I didn't expect the sun to reflect off the large shiny art structure out front. It blinds me and I don't see the distracted mound of muscle taking selfies in my path until it is too late.

We crash—my spaghetti arms to his massive chest, which is way too big for his shmedium T-shirt—and all thirteen books fall to the concrete.

I jump back in time to save my toes, but Muscles doesn't follow my lead. Instead, he fumbles for his precious phone as it tumbles to the ground with the books.

"Oww!" he screeches at a level reminiscent of Ms. Stanley's tiny dog when someone steps on his tiny paw. "What was that?"

"Books. Ever see one before?" I shouldn't have been so snarky, but Muscles is staring at me as if this disaster is all my fault. It's not like *he'll* have to pay for the harm done to this crumbled lot.

He lets out a sigh as he crouches and begins tossing said damaged books aside in a frantic search for his phone. When he locates it at the bottom of the pile, he brushes off a few harmless specs of dust before stomping past me, muttering a few choice insults under his breath.

"Right back at you," I growl, tucking away the incident as another blatant example of why I'm never dating again.

With a huff and a turn of my wrist, I check my watch. This reinforcement exercise has cut a chunk out of my book perusing time, which means I can't waste another minute with useless sulking. Plopping down to the sidewalk, I get busy reassembling the tower.

Hurried professionals in suits, sweaty joggers, and families of all sizes veer around me—all too busy to be bothered to help. Not that I need it. I can handle this little inconvenience on my own, I silently remind the universe, while examining the fresh scratches on the cover of the spicy rom-com I finished last night. Well, if I'm going to marry this book boyfriend soon, at least he knows how to treat a woman.

"You look like you could use a hand," someone says, and just my luck…a man.

"I've got it." After placing the last book on top of the stack, I push to my feet. But in straightening, the stack wobbles and lands in the arms of the one good Samaritan in this city.

"Doesn't seem like it," he says in an empathetic tone when I finally raise my eyes.

Damn. Why does he have to be good-looking and so…hot? Hotter than any fictional man I've ever conjured up in my overactive imagination. His brown eyes are dark, kind, and gazing into mine like I'm the first woman he's ever seen. It's intense and renders my self-preservation instincts null and void, as if I had no reason for them in the first place. But it isn't until the sun peeks through the clouds, highlighting his red shirt, that I recognize the warning signal. Red—as in slam on the mental brakes and stop these ridiculous thoughts of attraction.

"Well," I begin, snapping out of my trance and reaching for the books. "I carried them two blocks already, so…"

But he ignores my stubbornness and tosses a thumb over his impeccably toned and broad shoulder. "Can you believe that guy?"

"Who?"

"The guy in the cut-off T-shirt that bowled you over."

"Oh, right. Muscles." I huff out my frustration, and a chuckle blips out from between his lips. But he didn't seem the least bit embarrassed by it.

"Yeah, I guess so," he says almost as a question. "Who wears shirts like that? This isn't an 80's workout video."

"Right?" This guy is adorable. No. No, he isn't. He's still a man, and all men are to be avoided.

"So, where are you going with this library?"

I stare up at him and wait.

"Stupid question. Forget I said that."

"Too late."

He laughs again, hearty and smooth this time, and my stomach flutters. Traitor!

"I'm Will, by the way," he says and smiles. Not a full toothy smile, but a smug half grin like he was amused by something.

Is there salad in my teeth? Am I drooling at the large, tan bicep bulging under his sleeve from holding my books?

I shake out of the ogling. "What?"

"I said, I'm Will. Will Mason. What's your name?"

"Oh. Sydney Norman."

"Nice to meet you, Sydney. Can I carry this library to the library for you?"

"Sure," my mouth says before my brain has a chance to process a proper response. I look away, shocked that I'm allowing this little meeting to continue. As we set off down the sidewalk together, an inner dialogue of scolding and cursing is in full force.

"Which one was your favorite?" he says, pulling my attention back to him.

"Why? Are you looking for a recommendation?"

He twists his arm to scan the spines. "Not sure we have the same taste in books, but I'm interested in learning more about you."

"More? That implies that you already know something about me."

"I do." He flashes me a proud smile, and my stomach does that traitorous flutter again.

But as we come to my favorite fudge and milkshake shop, basic instinct has my eyes closing to properly take in the intoxicating scents before turning to face him. "All right, enlighten me," I challenge.

"Well, you obviously like fudge or at least the smell of it."

"Very observant."

"You like to read, and by the size of this pile, a lot. And…" he continues before I can interject, "you like to give people silly nicknames. That tells me you have a sense of humor. Do you have a nickname, Sydney?"

"Nope." Well, that's a lie. But since Trevor gave it to me, I'd prefer to pretend it doesn't exist.

"Did you give me a nickname?" he asks, all smooth and sensual, and I can't decide if I want to smack that smile off his face or smother him with kisses. Both sound quite satisfying.

"We just met," I say with a pop of my brow.

"You didn't know Muscles before, did you?"

"No, but his nickname was obvious."

I shift my weight to get my legs working, but all they want to do is stand here so my eyes can continue taking in this hunk of—nope. Not doing that.

He touches a long forefinger to his chin and sets his face to serious. "So, tell me. Which book was your favorite?"

Chapter Two

✰ ✰ ✰

Will

Sydney's looking up at me like I asked about the type of underwear she's wearing, and all I can think about is the color of her eyes. I've never seen that shade of green anywhere outside of the forest in springtime. They're brilliant, magical, expressive. I'm lost in their bottomless depths until someone steps out of the fudge shop and Sydney moves to let them pass.

"Is it a secret?" I finally ask so she'll refocus those eyes on me.

Her spontaneous laughter vibrates through the air, rippling over my skin as though she reached out and touched me. If only she had, so I could stop imagining what her soft skin might feel like on mine.

Her eyes take a quick roll. "It's not a secret."

"Or a difficult question. So you must be waiting to tell me later."

"What makes you think there will be a later?"

"You're still here, letting me carry your books."

She opens her mouth to say something. Then, her eyes narrow slightly like she's trying to figure me out. Shouldn't be hard. I'm an open book (pun intended). I smile at my unspoken joke, but when she stays silent, I tilt my head to get us moving again toward our destination.

I'm intrigued to see how much longer she can continue disregarding me. It doesn't happen often—although now that I think about it, it's never happened—and she's pricked my competitive side. Doesn't hurt that she's easy to look at. Her thick red hair falls in waves down her back and almost shimmers in the sun. She's petite, but not where it counts and her skin is like milk, smooth and flawless. I've never seen skin like hers, and the longer I'm with her, the more my hands itch to reach out. But those eyes of hers. There aren't words in the dictionary to describe them and what they do to me.

"If you won't tell me your favorite book from these, I'll just guess," I propose, hoping to keep her talking and my hands from misbehaving.

"Sure. But you only get three tries."

"Who says?" I protest, loving the banter and challenge. Rarely does a woman stimulate me as Sydney does. She's like a thousand-piece puzzle—fascinating, complicated, colorful.

"Time's running out. I can see the library from here."

"Damn." I bend to review the spines. "*A Light From You*?"

"Beautiful and sweet historical fiction by Ellison Lane. Great guess, but no cigar. Second guess?"

I peruse the titles again and roll my lips together at the irony. "Oh. I like the sound of this one. *Misbehaving*?"

"That's not a book about doing stupid or unlawful things."

"Shame."

"It's an economics book and really quite fascinating," she informs me, ignoring my comment. "But if you want to waste your turn with school-related books, that's—"

The next book to draw my attention is hot pink, and the title is interesting since it's probably how Sydney is feeling about me right now. "*My Own Best Enemy*?" I blurt out.

"Loved it and the author. Wasn't my favorite of this group. You lose."

She pokes out her bottom lip and gives me sad puppy eyes with a few dramatic blinks. I don't care how she looks at me so long as she keeps doing it.

"My favorite is *Meant To Be Us*," she finally answers and points to the black cover with bright green lettering.

"Why?"

"It had a little bit of everything—romance, adventure, intrigue, spice."

"Spice?" I ask, confused.

"Steamy moments."

"Steamy as in…"

"Sex." She says the word with such ease and a hint of an Irish accent that I almost drop the aforementioned spicy books.

"What's the matter? Did I make you uncomfortable with the S-word?"

Regaining my composure, I look over my shoulder and find her smirking, challenging me again. And that's when I notice our walk has slowed to a stroll. Interesting. "Nothing makes me uncomfortable," I inform her.

"Oh, really? Have a heart of steel? Lava in your veins? Wooden stomach?"

I laugh, which seems to happen a lot around her. "Not exactly. Marine. I'm trained to be unaffected by every situation." Except when I look into those deep emerald eyes of hers. No amount of training could prevent the chemical reaction that shoots off inside me like fireworks when I do.

"Military, huh? Active?"

"Yes. We're on leave for a long weekend."

"Are you based nearby?" she asks.

"Yeah, in Quantico, Virginia. But we're being deployed again soon."

"I heard troops were being sent overseas. How much longer do you have in the States?"

"Probably four to six months. But my buddy Jackson, our squad's sergeant, he's itching to get back. I wouldn't be surprised if he finds a way to get us shipped out tomorrow."

We stop in front of the library. Even at our turtle speed, we still reached our destination quicker than I would have preferred. She looks up at the building behind me, and I'm grateful when she doesn't head that way.

"Why does Jackson want to go so bad?"

"He loves serving, but he hates being home more."

"So, you're from Richmond?"

"Born and raised. You?" I ask, but she drops her gaze.

"No," is all she says.

Here it comes—the goodbye—and my gut clenches. What the hell? I don't get anxious, especially in this type of situation. Usually, the goodbye is my favorite part.

My brain flips into action, searching for a way to accomplish the mission my body has commanded: *Don't let her get away.* "After we drop off these books—"

"We?" she interrupts, catching my subtle clue.

"I carried them all this way. Any good gentleman would not just hand them over at this point."

"I carried them two blocks." Her arms cross indignantly. "You only had to endure one."

"Doesn't matter when it comes to the gentleman code. I wasn't there for those."

She stares at me for a moment then concedes. "Fine."

We begin climbing the tall flight of steps toward the front entrance. "As I was saying…after *we* drop off this mountain of books, how about I reward us with some fudge and a milkshake?"

"I don't think that's a good idea."

I pause between steps. "Why not?"

"Because you, Will Mason, are dangerous."

"I am no such thing. How is helping a beautiful woman carry her books dangerous?"

"Beautiful?" she asks, her brow raising a touch with amusement.

"I would have used stunning, but you caught me off guard."

"That." She points at me and holds back a smile. "That's why I can't go out with you."

"I didn't ask you out."

"Yes, you did."

"No," I contradict. "I said I'd treat us to some fudge and a milkshake after this hot trek. I, by no means, said a date." But now I wish I had.

"The answer's still no." With a spin, she continues up the steps.

At the top, she turns around to discover I haven't followed, and I swear something hard smacks against my chest. It isn't possible. I'm standing alone like a fool in a public area, but my heart stops on impact anyway when her eyes find mine.

Only for a moment, though, because a smile stretches her smooth, full lips and jolts me back to life. Electricity shoots through my veins, like a lightning bolt striking me with how badly I want to kiss her. Until now, I didn't know I could want something or someone so much it short circuits every cell in my body and overrides my thoughts. It's intoxicating.

"Are you coming, or did the word *no* knock the gentleman out of you?" A smirk touches her lips at the dig.

"That, Sydney Norman…" I sprint up the rest of the way, surprising her. "Is a word no woman has ever spoken to me, but there's always a first for everything."

She angles her head, studies me. "Are you a player, Will Mason?"

Standing this close, I can smell her shampoo—strawberry and vanilla—and have to fight the urge to bury my face in her long hair. To cover myself with the soft sweetness right here, right now.

Weak from the thought, all I can do is shake my head and mutter, "Gentleman," in protest.

Reflex has me sucking in a breath when she closes the distance between us, pressing her body to mine. She's at least seven inches shorter than me, but she commands my gaze, and I'm happy to oblige.

"Dangerous," she contradicts, and that's when I realize I've met my perfect match.

Chapter Three

✯ ✯ ✯

Sydney

Inside, Will waits in the nearby lobby while I complete the lengthy task of returning thirteen books. But it wouldn't take so long if I could stop myself from watching him as he strolled around from brochure rack to painting to window. His tall, muscular frame catches the attention of every female pair of eyes that happens upon him. And there seem to be only women in the library today. A lot of women.

It's entertaining to watch them fumble over themselves and marvel at their luck of coming on a day when Will Mason is there. They look him over and flirt with their lashes. Several even start a conversation.

Currently, the parade is brought to a halt while he talks with a tall, thin woman with perfect tan skin and thick golden hair that curls into wide spirals at the end. Every lock is sculpted with a purpose, like her legs and glutes, but she still manages to pull off the I-woke-up-like-this look in her high-end burgundy yoga pants and black tank.

But the show loses its entertainment value when Goldilocks reaches out to rest a hand on his arm. My stomach lurches at the sound of their simultaneous laughter, and again when he looks over her head and catches me watching. I yank my head back to the screen as if I'd been caught doing something shameful. It isn't my proudest moment, and I am ashamed. Just like the others in the parade, I couldn't tear my eyes away from him.

I'm weak, weakened by him, but that stops right now.

While he and Goldilocks are talking with her perfect hand perched on his perfect forearm, I sneak out the back door. I volunteered at the library through high school and am familiar with every inch, hidden nook, and escape route of that place. And an escape is exactly what I need before I, too, melt at his feet.

No. That can't happen. Correction…won't happen. Goldie can have him. They make a perfectly stunning couple.

I arrive for my shift at the bank both early and nauseous since I did some impressive speed-walking to get here. Anything to keep Will from spotting me if he somehow pulls himself away from the ogling. Listen to me, I huff to myself and pray my uneasy stomach isn't the result of unfounded jealousy. I have no right to feel that way. He can talk to whomever he wants. I don't care.

Besides, I've sworn off his species. They're nothing but trouble. And Will Mason is the king of trouble. It's written all over his gorgeous face.

At that, my body shudders instinctively, betraying me yet again.

"What's with the hard scowl?" Denise asks. Apparently, she had walked into the break room where I was recovering and witnessed my Will Mason hangover. She's never been one for subtleties, and I've always appreciated that about her…until now.

"Nothing."

"You're a bad liar. What happened? Meet a gorgeous sailor on the way to work?" Denise is a fan of any man in uniform, especially military.

Did I mention she also has a wild imagination and the uncanny ability to read minds?

I stare at her before caving. "Actually, a Marine."

"I knew it. There's only one thing that makes women talk to themselves in a disjointed trance. Plus, he's here."

Straightening in shock, I bang my shoulder against the old metal time clock hanging on the wall. The branch manager doesn't care for change or technology.

"What? He's here?" Why am I so frazzled?

Denise grins when I begin chewing my fingernail. "That's what I said, and he's asking for ya."

"How did he know?" Guess my secret escape wasn't so secret after all.

"Looks like you have…" She leans to the side to check the clock behind me. "About ten minutes to go find that out. And if you add this one to your ridiculous no-date list, can I have him?" She bites her lip, and I feel a twinge of possessiveness wash over me. Okay, it's more than a twinge. It's a fire hose soaking my skin and weighing me down.

And precisely why this has to stop.

"Sure. I'll give him your number."

Feeling lighter and full of resolve, I step past her and stalk toward the lobby. But then I see him, standing in front of a window, and I'm weakened once again. A stream of sunlight highlights him like a spotlight, tracing every inch into an impressive masculine shadow on the floor. He's holding something that looks like a rose, but not an ordinary one.

I can't take my eyes off it—off him—and didn't notice him strolling toward me until he spoke.

"You left without saying goodbye."

I blink hard and shake my head to reset my thoughts. "I'm sorry," I say lamely. "I needed to get to work, and you were preoccupied." Did I really just say that and in a tone that screams I didn't like him being *preoccupied* with someone other than me? "How did you find me?"

"I asked the sweet lady at the front desk if she saw where you went. Apparently, she did and was willing to share more than just your escape route."

Betty is going to hear a thing or two about that next time I see her. What if Will is a serial killer or a stalker?

"This is for you." He holds up the stiff flower, and then I understand why it looks different. It's made with a paper flyer. And not just any flyer—the library's romance novel monthly recommendations list. I'd recognize it anywhere since I used to help create it, and it's always printed on red paper.

"Will," I manage but don't take his gift. "I can't go out with you. I won't."

"I didn't ask you to go out with me."

"Then what's this for?"

"Because I think you're stunning and funny and interesting."

That wilts any determination I built up on the way here, and I curse myself silently. "Did you make it?"

"Does it matter?"

"Yes."

"Okay. I made it," he answers flatly, holding my gaze.

"Did you really or are you just trying to get me to take it?"

"Take the darn flower," the older woman sitting on the couch behind me urges with frustration. "Can't you see he's smitten?"

I whip my head around. "Maybe I don't want him to be smitten," I growl between gritted teeth.

"Why not, dearie? Look at him."

Unable to stop myself, I turn back but don't like what I see. Smitten isn't the way I'd describe the look in his dark chocolate eyes. His look is something the book boyfriends invented and he perfected.

"Thank you." My voice is hoarse as I reach out. My pinky finger brushes against his hand and tingles of varying magnitudes shoot up my arm. They travel down my spine and send goosebumps over my legs. Damn you, meddling old lady number two.

I try to pull the flower from his grasp, but he holds on. "Have dinner with me tonight," he demands and lets the stem slide from his fingers.

"I thought you weren't asking me out."

"That was earlier. This is now. Ingrid is right. I'm—"

"Who's Ingrid?"

"That's me, dearie," meddling old lady number two clarifies.

"You two know each other?" I ask her.

"We chatted while you kept him unnecessarily waiting."

Rolling my eyes, I return my attention to Will and let out a long exhale. "What is *Ingrid* right about?"

"I'm smitten and want to see you again."

I smile, unable to stop it. He is so damn adorable. And forward. And unmistakably male. Ignoring my overstimulated heart, I shake my head. "I can't."

"Oh, for goodness' sake." Ingrid shoots out of her seat faster than her frail body should allow. "I'll go out with you, sweetie," she says to Will, placing a wrinkled hand on his arm. What is it with females touching him all the time? "She's either too stubborn or too dumb to waste your time on."

"Hey!" I protest and Ingrid laughs.

"If you're going to let him get away, you're dumber than you look."

"I like her," Will adds after Ingrid shuffles off.

"The answer's still no. Thank you for the flower, and I hope you stay safe during your next deployment."

"I'm not giving up," he calls after me as I flee once more, and I can't help hoping that he doesn't.

―――

Sydney's Journal

April 16th

Mark my words...Will Mason is trouble. Like the urge to stare at the sun even though you know it'll be blinding, eating <u>one</u> more chunk of fudge, or downing that third shot of tequila that sends you into drunken bliss. Nothing good comes after those things.

On the way to the library today, I was minding my own business when BAM, Will Mason flipped my world upside down. This is after I had already SLAMMED into a despicable representation of the male species...the opposite of Will Mason. Thankfully, that despicable sample was enough to remind me that I don't date. I don't want my life rocked by a sexier-than-a-book-boyfriend Marine who makes my insides quiver.

I'm saying NO and writing it down, so I'll actually stick to it. They say (whoever 'they' are) that if you write it down, there's a better chance it will happen.

So, let it be known, world: WILL MASON WILL NOT BREAK ME.

There.

Chapter Four

✯ ✯ ✯

Will

"What's on your mind?" Jackson asks as we linger over a six-pack on the back deck of Billy's parents' house. It's late, and no matter how many cans I drain, I can't seem to get a certain redhead out of my thoughts.

"Nothing. When do you want to head back to base?"

Jackson narrows his eyes at me, not buying my attempt to redirect the conversation. But thankfully, he plays along. "Monday after lunch. We've got an early morning on Tuesday."

"What day doesn't start early with you?"

"True."

"How many miles did you clock today?" I ask, lifting the beer can to my lips.

Jackson's second passion, behind serving, is running. He can run twice as long and do more push-ups and sit-ups than the best athlete at the base. I guess you could say he *is* the best athlete at the base and probably in the entire Marine Corps. If he hadn't been my best friend since kindergarten, I'd despise him—especially when he has us run every mile with him at an ungodly hour every morning.

"Twenty-one."

"I hate you."

"So, where were you this afternoon?" Jackson asks, then drains the last of his beer before setting the empty can on the table. "I thought you were going with me?"

"Yeah, sorry about that. I got held up downtown."

"Doing what?"

When an excuse isn't on the tip of my tongue, he's quick to call me out. "Who was she, or do you not remember?"

"Very funny."

"Billy and Josh are going to be furious with you," he accuses.

"Why?"

"You know they like to be your wingman."

My hand waves pointlessly in the air, dismissing his statement. "Wasn't like that."

"So, there was a woman." Jackson smirks.

"Maybe." I wink and prop my feet up on the opposite chair. "I'll make it up to them tomorrow night." It's Billy's birthday, and we're all going out to celebrate. "How was lunch with Eleanor?"

"Great. She sends her love."

"She still mad that you're staying here and not at the estate?" I ask. Eleanor manages Jackson's father's house and the surrounding grounds. She cooks, cleans, mows the lawn, gardens, does the maintenance, all of it. She even raised Jackson since his parents were too busy to give him the time of day. Which was fine with Jackson and the rest of us since his father is a colossal ass.

"She'll be fine," he answers. "Plus, Grayson's having one of his corporate dinner parties there tonight. He wouldn't want his only son ruining his fun or reputation."

"Which rich bastard's wife is he fucking this week?"

"Hell if I know." Jackson yanks another beer from the cooler and flips up the tab to open it. "Don't care either. I'm just glad I don't have to see it."

"Amen, brother." I hold up my beer in salute before draining it. "What are you doing before Billy's birthday shindig?"

"Shindig?"

"Whatever."

"Nothing much," Jackson answers. "I promised Eleanor that I'd help her with a few things at the house."

"After Grayson leaves, I assume."

"Of course. Since I'm here, the least I can do is help her put the house back together since he won't. What about you?"

My hand immediately glides over my short hair. No good reasons for going downtown again came to mind, but I have to see Sydney again. She's all I think about. "I have a few errands to run. Nothing exciting," I say lamely.

Jackson scoffs. "Right."

"What?"

"Since when do you call sex an errand." He air-quotes the word with his fingers.

"Errands are chores," I correct. "I would never call sex a chore."

"No, you definitely wouldn't. Well, I hope you enjoy your *errands*."

"Oh, I definitely will."

―――――

Although I try not to think about her, I lie awake half the night, putting together a plan to convince Sydney to say yes to a date. I already know when her shift begins today at the bank—her co-worker was quick to divulge that information in her absence.

I'll start by cornering her there again. That seemed to soften her a little, or maybe by that point yesterday, I'd already worn her down. She isn't easily flustered or swayed, which is both sexy and frustrating at the same time. The guy that messed her up must have been a prolific jerk—another Grayson. For his sake, I hope we don't cross paths.

After a shower and breakfast with my parents (Jackson was already gone since he rises at the ass-crack of dawn), I head downtown in my rusty two-seater truck from high school to accomplish a very important mission.

According to the intel I gathered yesterday, Sydney works at the bank drive-thru on Saturdays. Since I can't exactly talk to her, I'll need a little creativity, which is why I was up half the night. But I'm satisfied with the final plan, and I'm ready to execute it.

Upon arrival at the rendezvous point (4.23 miles southwest of home base), I slip into undercover status and drive around the sturdy brick building undetected. From behind my favorite aviator sunglasses, I survey the area and discover my beautiful target situated behind a wide window in lane number one. Three vehicles are already idling there, but no other obstacles as far as I can tell. The sky is clear with a slight spring wind, and Sydney's wearing a friendly smile. Conditions are favorable for a smooth and swift victory.

Satisfied, I join in line and prepare to initiate contact.

While I wait, I scribble a note on a deposit slip and select a flower from the bouquet I picked up on the way. If a personalized paper flower didn't do the trick, maybe real ones will soften her reluctance. But I purchased the largest bouquet I could find at the grocery store in case the first attempt goes as I expect, requiring multiple attempts to achieve the goal.

When it's my turn, my stomach revs with the engine as I press on the gas. But hope quickly deflates when I pull up to find her seat empty. This can't be happening. I thought of everything. Well, everything except a back-up plan. What if another teller takes over her station? I'll have to abandon the original mission and regroup.

A minute passes while I idle at the window and brainstorm alternative actions. But I'm saved from it all when she reappears behind the glass. And adding to this crazy scheme is her total disregard for her new customer. She's distracted and pushes the button to release the tray without noticing me.

Anticipation is building as I place the note and flower in the tray. From my vantage point, I have a full view of her and enjoy how her face shifts from tired annoyance to confusion to shock.

Her gaze rises to mine and holds for a beat like she's figuring out her next move. Then, curiosity takes the trophy when she lowers her eyes to read the note. She looks it over, biting back a grin, before writing something on the slip in reply. Then, she lifts the pink daisy to her nose and pushes the tray back out.

I can't tear my eyes from her. The clear, mid-morning sky reflects off the glass and centers her in a blue and white halo. She removes the blossom from her face to reveal a sweet smile, and I forget why I'm there in the first place.

It's dangerous to lose your bearings, disregard your surroundings, and ignore the people around you. Training has beat that into my head. It rules my life whether I'm in uniform or not—until she comes into view.

But I'm reminded of the mission when Sydney points the flower toward the open tray, her amused expression filling the silence. I can almost hear her laughter. It lives on repeat in my thoughts.

Retrieving the note, I read her neat handwritten response:

Still no. Thank you for the flower.

Undeterred by the rejection, it was expected after all, I flash a wink and drive off to rejoin the line. Time for tactic number two.

As the line inches forward, I write my next note:

I challenge you to a fudge bake-off. My place (parents will be home, so you don't have to worry about being molested). I'll pick you up after work.

This time, she's sitting behind the window when I roll up. She tilts her head in playful disapproval of my antics but pushes the tray out anyway. If I didn't know better, I'd say she is enjoying this merry-go-round flirting operation. She's making me work for that yes and is probably still convinced she won't give it. But she's about to figure out that I'm not easily dissuaded.

She reads the note with a smirk, then crafts a response with one hand while holding the two new flowers in the other. When she sends the note back through, hope is building. Her smile is different. Maybe her response will be, too.

I snatch it from the tray and read her answer:

You don't bake fudge, and I'm a terrible cook.

Defeated again, I look up, and she waves me on. There's a long line of impatient customers behind me. I nod and take off again, prepared to try one more time. The bank closes in an hour, and if she turns me down again, I'll just wait her out. To clarify, I'm not a stalker. I'm simply persistent when I see something I want.

My final note says:

What if we meet at the library to read or play chess? No talking. No touching. No pressure.

Her response:

What fun is that?

An answer I can appreciate. All right, an after-work, in-person intercept it is. We'll see if she can resist me when there's no glass and an aggravated line of customers between us.

An hour later, she strolls out of the bank, stopping short when she sees me at the bottom of the steps, holding the rest of the bouquet. I'm encouraged by the six familiar flowers in her hand. She didn't throw them away or give them to someone else. Or worse yet, toss them in the trash. They touched her enough to keep them. Hope is mounting in full construction mode now.

"What are you doing here?" she asks from the top of the stoop, and I have to admit it's a good question. The last thing I should be doing is getting involved with someone this close to deployment. But I have no restraint where she's concerned.

"Well, you apparently don't like any of my date ideas, so I thought I'd walk you home—like a gentleman. You shouldn't be walking home alone at this hour."

"It's one o'clock in the afternoon."

"Very dangerous."

"You're dangerous," she jokes and joins me on the sidewalk.

"Are these dangerous?" I hold up the rest of the bouquet, making her laugh.

"No."

"Then, you'll keep them and think of me?"

Her eyelashes flutter as she considers the question. "Maybe."

"Good enough for me." I hand her the bouquet, and she inserts the others into the center. "I also got you this," I say in a near whisper, holding up a small plastic bag. She makes basic functions difficult to muster.

"What is it?"

I reach inside and pull out a little white box. There's a gold sticker with a logo securing the top, and she recognizes it instantly.

"No way?!"

After I open it, she leans over to see the contents inside. "I thought you might be hungry."

She breathes deep. "I'm always hungry for fudge."

"Noted."

She raises her eyes in disapproval before reaching inside. "Where's yours?"

"Funny. I figured we'd share, but if you want to eat an entire pound of fudge, I'm up for seeing you try." But I'd watch her do anything at this point.

"Don't dare me, Mason. I've downed a lot more than a pound of fudge in my day. The Irish are professional drinkers…and eaters," she adds, her subtle Irish accent slipping into her words again, and I almost trip over my own feet.

"Oh, really?" I say recovering. "Maybe I should have brought shepherd's pie instead."

She snatches the box out of my hand. "Don't even think it. You did good."

"Thanks. Speaking of drinking, my friends and I are going out tonight. If you were to go out too and randomly pick the same bar, I'd be okay with that."

"Randomly?" she teases and hands me a large fudge square.

"I was wondering if you were going to loosen your grip on that."

"Almost didn't."

I'm about to toss the square into my mouth but hesitate when I notice her eyeing me with a smirk. "What?"

"That won't be the best decision you've made today."

"What? Eating this?" I hold up the fudge. "Isn't that what it's for?"

Her eyes roll back with a sigh. "Trust me. You don't want to eat that entire chunk all at once."

"Why not?"

"Small bites, big—never mind. Go for it."

I study her, then accept the challenge, popping the chunk into my mouth. As we walk, she tries to hide her amusement while waiting for me to admit she was right. Which I would never do…if I could talk. All I can do is chew the gooey chocolate and caramel. And chew and chew. There seems to be more caramel than fudge in my piece. It's stuck to the top of my mouth and in my teeth. And I'm thirsty. So very thirsty. What I wouldn't give for a glass of water to dissolve all this sugar.

"How's the fudge?" she asks, but I can't open my mouth enough to answer. It's like wet cement at this point.

"Here." Graciously, she removes a bottle of water from her bag and opens it. I knew I liked her for a reason.

After downing half of it, I toss up a thumb. "It's fantastic," I manage and swallow the last of the chocolate-flavored caramel goo.

"Don't you have something else to say, tough guy?"

I stare down at her. "No idea what you're talking about."

"Fine. It's satisfying enough to know you were thinking it. You have a terrible poker face." She nudges me with her shoulder, and I stumble off course. "But you're pretty cute when you surrender."

"I seem to be doing that a lot lately, thanks to you."

"That's pretty dramatic."

"It's what you and your sexy eyes do to me." I watch her blush, loving the color on her cheeks, then circle back to the other reason I showed up today. "So, about that non-date random bar appearance."

"This is me." She stops in front of an apartment complex, ignoring my second attempt to make plans for tonight.

Behind her is a three-story brick motel-like building that looks original to the 1950s. Nothing has been updated or maintained for decades. The pale-yellow apartment doors are rusted, and several of the windows are boarded with crumbling plywood. I don't want to leave her here alone. The area and the dilapidated structure look anything but safe.

"Will I see you later?" I persist, but she dodges again.

"Thank you for the fudge and the gentlemanly escort."

Why does she keep doing that?

"Sydney," I plea and take her hand before I think better of it. But she doesn't pull away. Instead, she laces her fingers with mine, and I swear I see her breath catch in her chest.

"Will," she whispers when I step closer. "This isn't a good idea."

"Why?"

"You're leaving soon, which doesn't matter because I've sworn off men. Especially dangerous ones."

She smiles, but because it's shaky and she won't look at me, my blood heats up. She's hiding and scared of getting hurt again. Of losing a part of herself.

"I'm not the idiot that hurt you and let you go." My free hand needs to touch her. Needs to remove the pain in her eyes. I brush my knuckles lightly over her cheek and lower my head. Testing. Wanting. I'm close enough now to feel her breath hot on my lips, teasing me and making me come undone.

She presses against me, and that's when I realize she's not pushing me away. Not distracting me from going after what I want. She's giving herself freely. With my eyes locked on hers, I cup her face with both hands. Her hands move to my waist and the electricity between us could light a match. We might set this entire lot ablaze with one kiss.

"Are you sure about this," I ask, giving her a way out if she needs one. But now that she's in my hands, not touching her seems like an impossible option. "Say the word and—"

"Just shut up and kiss me."

Hearing the best answer ever is all it takes to make me lightheaded with desire. But as I lower to take what we both want, she jumps back and screams.

"What is it?" I ask, searching her face for an explanation. She's frantic but smiling.

"Mr. Darcy!"

"Who?"

She bursts into what I can only describe as a congested, hyena laugh. "Mr. Darcy, my neighbor's chihuahua," she explains through the high-pitched snickers and deep nose snorts.

I look down and see the tiny dog scoot around our feet, then zigzag across the grass. I want to be annoyed at the so-called dog for ruining the moment, but the sound of her contradicting laughter—laugh, snort, laugh, snort—is too contagious and, somehow, sexy.

"Grab him," she yells when he sprints toward me.

I lunge at the dog, but he slips through my fingers. Grasping at air takes me off balance, and I drop to a knee to keep from falling on my face.

"That was graceful," she teases.

"It would be a lot easier if he wasn't the size of a rat."

"Don't let him get to the sidewalk. Ms. Stanley will be out here soon, and she won't be happy if we let him get away."

"And how do you propose I do that? He's like a little rocket ship."

She folds over in another fit of laughter. When I realize she's laughing at me, I sprint toward her—rogue rat rocket forgotten. She squeals and takes off, but I'm faster. I wrap an arm around her waist and lift her off her feet.

"This will teach you to laugh at me."

"Oh, yeah? What are you going to do?" She kicks and squirms when I dig my fingers into her side. "No! Not that!"

Everything is going to plan until she slides out of my grasp. I try to catch her, but in breaking her fall, I collapse on top of her.

There are worse places to be.

I can feel the shape of her body under me. She isn't lacking in any of the places that make a man's blood percolate. Sultry features that demand attention and make anyone within eye shot take notice of.

And I'll be the first to admit...I've noticed. A lot. And now I *feel* her feminine landscape, where it rises and falls and curves like a country road. My hand reaches for her bare thigh, and the way her skin shimmers under the gentle touch has my pulse doing the same. Except the electric current isn't just making its presence known. It's bouncing off every nerve in my body and creating a variety of ungentlemanly thoughts.

She must be feeling the same or something similar because her breathing is shallow and rapid, making her chest press against mine on each ragged inhale. And she isn't laughing anymore.

I brush the hair that had blown into her face and kiss the gentle angle of her jawline. "You're going to be the end of me," I whisper.

"Then, you might as well go out with a bang."

Chapter Five

★ ★ ★

Sydney

I have no idea what came over me. I shouldn't have given in to those dark, come-hither-I-have-fudge eyes and kissed him. Especially since I already know that they make me do stupid things like allow him to walk me home, hold his hand, and show him how he affects me. It's only encouraging him, and nothing good can come from this behavior. But my goodness, he's irresistible. And what's worse? His kiss is flipping my brain into full-on stupid mode.

Maybe it's just my body reacting to an attractive man desiring me again. But it doesn't feel that simple. In fact, it feels complicated, extraordinary, rare. And foolish me, I don't want that feeling to end.

This isn't me. I don't go into situations like this blindly, but my willpower—the one keeping me from not dragging him upstairs to my apartment—is fading.

"Will," I attempt to put some sense into the situation, but he deepens the kiss.

This is wrong. I know it is, but I'm glad he did it. Glad he dug in and shocked my heart back to life. It's been working right above dormant behind a locked fortress of impenetrable steel since I pieced myself back together late last year.

Despite months of self-rehab, therapy sessions with Nora, and many bottles of wine, my heart's still fragile. I need to protect it. But how can I when he feels this good and so incredibly more than anticipated? My leg wraps around him, pulling him closer. A low moan escapes my throat when his tongue brushes mine, and I'm not thinking about what that reveals. I don't care that every inch of my body is connected to and trembling under a hunky stranger while we lie in the grass in broad daylight. I've forgotten about—

"Oww," I manage and push on Will's firm chest. Shock rushes over me from the fortress-matching feel of his muscles and how each one is on alert. I pause in admiration before refocusing on the source of the pain.

"What was that?"

"My foot. Something bit—Oh, no!" I sit up, reluctantly rolling Will off me, and look around. Ms. Stanley should be chasing after Mr. Darcy right now, but there's only an empty lot and a hysterical chihuahua. "Something's wrong."

"Nothing about this feels wrong."

I smack him on the shoulder. "I mean, Mr. Darcy's still here, and his owner isn't. She's usually a minute behind him."

"I'm sure she's on her way."

"No. You don't understand. She should be here. Mr. Darcy means everything to her."

"Alright. Do you want to go check on her?"

I nod. "Grab Mr. Darcy and meet me upstairs."

Hopping to his feet, he pulls me up. But instead of rushing after the dog, he wraps me in a hug and kisses my head. "I'll be right behind you. What's the apartment number?"

"213," I answer, grateful he's here.

"Take your bag in case you need to call 9-1-1."

"Good idea."

When I reach Ms. Stanley's apartment on the second floor, the door is open, but only wide enough for one little chihuahua to dash through it. I call out to her and push on the door, but it won't open more than a few inches. I call again and bang my palm against the old metal. No answer. Something's blocking the door. Concern for her safety has me retrieving my phone and dialing 9-1-1 as Will suggested.

"Yes. I'm at 709 Smithfield Avenue, apartment number 213. My neighbor isn't responding, and I'm worried something's wrong. She's a diabetic and sometimes spacey with her food and medication. No, I don't know about that. The door won't open. Yes. Thank you. Hurry."

I throw my phone into the bag and go back to banging on the door. By the time Will shows up, my hyperactive heart is pounding louder in my ears than the sound of my palm on the metal. I look over, and Mr. Darcy is snuggled safely inside Will's hand, and I can't stop myself from wishing for the same treatment.

"I don't know what to do," I admit and pace to the balcony rail while Will checks the door. Traffic on the major thoroughfare in front of our complex is lighter than usual at this time of day, and the sky is bright blue and clear. But none of that registers. Ms. Stanley is in trouble, and Will's standing nearby, being supportive and adorable.

Turning to watch him, I can't believe he's still here. He's evaluating the apartment, looking through the window, examining the door hinges, all to find a solution. He doesn't know Ms. Stanley, but he's trying to help, wants to help. Then, Mr. Darcy barks and my thoughts switch to what happened downstairs…what might have happened had a pesky dog not intervened.

Heat burns my cheeks at how I reacted. I let the situation get out of hand and now it's going to be even harder to send him away. He won't understand why I've been so hot one minute and cold the next, but that's not my concern. I need to focus on what's best for me in the long run and help Ms. Stanley now. I turn, planning to tell him to leave, when he speaks first.

"Medics on their way?"

"Yes, but—"

He passes over Mr. Darcy. "I'm going in."

"You're what?"

He points to the dusty window. "She's on the floor behind the door. That's why it won't open." He begins walking backward. "I'm going to try the back door."

"How? There's no fire escape."

"There's no…?" On an audible exhale, his fingers spring to the base of his nose to pinch the bone between his eyes. "Wait here."

"Will!" But he's already running down the balcony toward the stairs. I look down at Mr. Darcy. "What's he going to do, scale the brick?"

What feels like only seconds later, a loud bang echoes over the building before I hear footsteps inside the apartment. The door soon creaks open, evidence that Will somehow found a way in and shifted Ms. Stanley aside. I rush inside and push the door closed with my foot.

"Oh my God." I drop to my knees and let Mr. Darcy wiggle free. Will's already on the other side of her, checking for a pulse.

"Does she have any illnesses? Has she passed out before?" he asks quickly.

"She's a diabetic and not great with—"

Will jumps up and begins rummaging through the drawers of the end tables beside the couch.

"What are you doing?"

"Looking for glucagon. Do you know where she keeps it?" He moves to the kitchen, and I follow with Mr. Darcy on my heels.

"No. I don't even know what that is."

"She's probably hypoglycemic." He opens the last drawer, then reaches inside for a narrow orange container and opens it. "Found it."

"Found wha—is that a syringe?"

"Yes." He inserts the needle into a little bottle and slowly pulls out the plunger. Tossing the bottle aside, he shakes the syringe and grabs a pre-packaged alcohol wipe from the kit. "Come on. I need your help."

Too stunned and panicked to ask questions or think for myself, I follow him back to Ms. Stanley and drop to the floor opposite him. He rips open the package with his teeth, removes the towelette, and begins wiping it over Ms. Stanley's upper right arm. "Hold up her sleeve."

After grabbing the soft fabric of her bright blue shirt with chihuahua-sized black dog paws printed all over, I watch in awe as Will inserts the needle into her arm. "Are you sure this is going to help?"

"No," he answers flatly before reaching under her and rolling her over to face me. "But if I'm right, she should wake up by the time the medics get here."

"How do you know all this?"

"Both my grandparents, my mother's side of the family, were diabetics. Before I joined the military, I'd stop by and check on them after practice or school."

"Practice?"

"The boys and I played football."

"Do you do everything with *the boys*?"

"Well, not *everything*." He winks, and despite myself, I blush.

"Thank goodness. I was beginning to worry about your decision-making skills."

He sets aside the syringe and crawls over Ms. Stanley to sit beside me. "So, I saved the rat-dog from certain doom. I kicked down a door like a real man."

"Mmmm." I figure I know where this list of good deeds is going. "How did you do that, by the way? We're on the second floor and there are no stairs or deck to the back door. You haven't been bitten by any spiders lately, have you?"

A smug grin turns up the corners of his lips. "Unfortunately, no. Just the rat." He holds up his hand and points to the inside base of his thumb. "We had to have a little…discussion earlier."

I gasp at the four red puncture marks in his skin. "But he was so calm when you came upstairs."

"That was *after* the discussion." He shrugs. "We're buds now."

Nothing could have prevented the unexpected laugh-snort combination that popped out of me. I slap a hand over my mouth to prevent another one and stare at him with wide eyes. But instead of poking fun at me or crinkling his nose in disgust at the non-lady-like sound as my ex did, Will's dark eyes soften, and he smiles—a sweet, adoring, appreciative smile that settles me and keeps my cheeks from matching my red hair.

But when he reaches out and presses on my forearm, my insides heat up like a furnace for a different reason. His gaze never leaves mine as my fingers slowly slide from my lips and into his hand.

"Don't ever hide who you are, Sydney."

It's impossible to muster anything more than a nod when he's looking at me like that. But I have to do something. He's watching me, waiting. So, I do the only thing I can. I ignore the danger sirens going off in my head and snuggle up against him.

"As I was saying," he starts to break the silence, and I imagine, to also lighten the mood. "Rat-dog was saved and won over." He holds up a finger.

"Check," I say to play along.

"Real man test complete."

"Passed with flying colors."

He snickers, then unfolds two more fingers. "I brought you fudge and enough for seconds tomorrow."

"My hero."

"That makes me a hero? Not scaling the wall and breaking down a door that probably hadn't been opened since 1953?"

I laugh. God, I'm in trouble. "And flowers. Don't forget the flowers," I say to keep from pulling him closer right here in Ms. Stanley's apartment.

"Oh, yeah. And I let you kiss me."

"Let me?" I sit up to face him squarely. "As I recall, you tackled me in broad daylight."

"But you were the one who said to, and I quote, 'Shut up and kiss me'."

I quickly return to the warm, cozy spot beneath his arm when a cringe threatens to roll over my face. There's no denying it…I said it.

"I know what you're thinking," he says when I can't conjure up a reply.

"What am I thinking?"

"That you enjoyed our first kiss more than you expected, and you're curious if it will be that hot a second time."

A grin threatens, so I pinch it back. "Don't flatter yourself."

"Don't have to. Your body did all the talking."

The feel of his soft lips and my chemical reaction to them flood my thoughts. I should be embarrassed by the way I threw myself at him, especially after telling him I don't date. How does that make me look? I know exactly how it looks, and for the first time, I wonder if that's why he's interested in me. Does he think I'd be an easy conquest before he leaves? That with all my damage and relationship insecurities, he can charm me, then sneak away in the night, never to be heard from again? Maybe he's good at the game. Good at making women feel special, like they're the only person that matters in his world. Like they're finally understood and seen, so they'll fall at his feet and into his bed.

Even thinking that might be true sends a chill down my back. He must feel the tension enter my body because he places his free hand under my chin and tilts my face. I have no option but to meet his gaze.

"Whatever you're thinking now, don't," he says gently.

I swallow the lump forming in my throat. "You don't know what I'm thinking. Maybe I'm considering kissing you again, and you just told me not to."

Ignoring my unsteady joke, he twists to take both my hands, forcing me to sit up. "Meet me at Backseat tonight. The guys and I are going there for Billy's birthday. I want to see you again."

My head shakes in answer before I can find the words. "I can't trust me around you, and I don't know you well enough to trust you either."

"What's not to trust?"

When I don't join in the banter, his face drops, and I hate myself for it.

"Sydney, why don't you tell me what's bothering—" He stops when Ms. Stanley groans.

I push to my feet and grab the blanket off the recliner to place under her head. "Ms. Stanley, it's Sydney. Are you okay?"

She rolls her head from side to side, and my chest tightens when a tear escapes her eye.

"Ms. Stanley, you passed out. The ambulance should be here soon to help."

She opens her eyes and focuses on Will, her brow pinching in the middle.

"That's Will. He gave you a shot of—" I look at him for assistance.

"Glucagon," he provides.

"Looks like that's what you needed."

She gives a little nod and reaches for Will with her free hand. He takes it and lifts her fingers to his lips. I try not to melt at the sweet gesture, but my body is still a traitor.

"They're here," I say when I hear sirens approaching outside. But before I can move, Will places a hand on my arm to stop me.

"I'll get them."

Chapter Six

✦ ✦ ✦

Sydney

As we watch the medics load Ms. Stanley onto the ambulance, Will takes my hand. "You did well," he says. But the feel of his hand is confusing right and wrong, and it has to stop.

Still convincing myself, I slide my hand from his and blurt out, "This can't continue," before I lose the nerve. But he turns toward me with hurt in his eyes, and I fight the urge to take it back.

"Why? I like you."

I shove my hands in the back pockets of my corduroy skirt to keep them from reaching for him. "I know, but—"

"I thought we were finally on the same page. I kicked down a door for you," he adds with a smirk.

"Don't do that," I demand.

"Do what?"

"Be adorable."

Before I can react, he steps forward and takes my face in his hands again. I suck in what feels like my last breath as his lips cover mine. His grip is intentional, but his kiss is tender and sweet. Patient like he's waiting for me to change my mind.

I won't.

Yanking myself away, I stumble back, my knees too weak from his touch to handle the abrupt movement. "I have to go," I say on an exhale and take off. "I'm sorry."

It was cowardly. But running was easier than continuing to face him, disappoint him, hurt him.

———

Sydney's Journal

April 17th

I need help. I've been reading through old journal entries, hoping to remind myself why I'm single. Why I've sworn off men despite how they make me feel. But it's not fixing my Will Mason problem.

He's nothing like Trevor or any other man I've met or dated, for that matter. He's thoughtful and sweet. He's confident without being arrogant. He goes out of his way to show me he cares. He's funny and sexy as hell.

I feel horrible for rejecting him. But now that he's gone, shouldn't I feel better? Shouldn't it be a relief to know I won't have to be tempted by him any longer? But I know where to find him—tonight anyway—and that's been haunting me. He haunts me, and it hurts. Hurts worse than it did when I ran away.

And wasn't that embarrassing?

But I'll get over it. Minutes, hours, and days will pass, and I'll forget about him. It may not feel like it now, but I will be glad I stayed on course. Glad I didn't fall for him and subject myself to more heartache. Because that's all relationships are. Soul-crushing, gut-wrenching, never-the-same again heartache.

And I can't go there a second time. No matter how thoughtful, sweet, special, funny, and sexy as hell he may be.

No. I can't go there.

"Why are you so crabby?" Nora asks when I snap at her a second time.

"Men."

"What men? You're not dating anyone." She sits on the edge of the bed. "Did Trevor show his ugly face again?"

I shake my head as tears coat my cheeks.

"Sweetie, talk to me. Why are you upset?"

"Good question."

"What does that mean?" she asks, and I wish I had an inkling of how to explain it.

"I met someone."

"You did? Where?"

"Yesterday. It's a long story, but he ended up carrying my books to the library and following me to work." I glance at the flower he made resting on my dresser, and Nora follows my gaze.

"I was wondering where that came from. What's his name?" she asks.

"Will. He makes me weak. I've never been kissed like he—"

"You kissed him?!"

I grimace remembering my reaction to him in the grass. "Yeah."

"And it was hotter than hot, huh?"

"Yeah."

"And…you're crying because…" she asks in that therapist way of hers.

"I lost control, and I'm afraid he only wants me for sex," I wail like a heartbroken teenager. Again, not one of my finest moments.

She waits for me to compose myself before continuing. "And that's a problem because…"

I glare at her. Doesn't she know me better than this? She's my best friend, therapist, and roommate. She understands me better than anyone.

"Sorry, I'm so confused," she says, tossing her hands up before letting them drop to her lap.

"Nora, he's gorgeous and sweet and attentive. He's hilarious and witty. He brought me fudge and flowers and saved Mr. Darcy and knocked in a door to help Ms. Stanley and kissed her hand." Messy tears continue to drench my face, but Nora doesn't seem to notice.

"I'm going to need more explanation on some of that, but Sydney, he sounds amazing." She smooths my unruly hair, then dries my cheeks with a fresh tissue she snatched from the box on my bed.

"He is." I fall back onto my pillow with a loud sniff. "He wants me to meet him at Backseat tonight."

"That's great. Why aren't you getting ready?"

"He's a Marine."

"So?" Nora lies on her side to join me.

"He has to return to the base, and he's expecting to be deployed soon."

"Even more reason to go tonight."

I shoot up and stare down at her. "What? That's the biggest reason *not* to go."

"I disagree."

"Explain."

Sitting up, she takes my hands. She does that when she wants to ensure I'm listening. "You kissed this guy after knowing him for less than a few hours. That's not like you." She holds up a hand to stop my complaint. "I know what you're thinking. You're not a slut for doing it. It happened because he makes you comfortable, and when you're comfortable, you let the real Sydney come out. I hate to break it to you. The real Sydney is pretty amazing *and* irresistible. I actually feel sorry for the guy."

I manage a grin. I can always count on Nora to have my back. "But what if I get attached and he forgets about me while he's away?"

"Not possible. But if the universe crumbles and that actually happens, then you have some amazing memories with a gorgeous man. You're twenty-two, Sydney. No one says you have to marry the guy. Let yourself have some fun, enjoy the orgasms, and see what happens."

"Nora!"

"What?" She flashes an innocent grin, but she's never been shy where sex is concerned. "Great sex doesn't only happen in your romance novels. Answer me this. He's been pursuing you pretty hard, hasn't he?"

"Relentlessly and in the most adorable ways."

"And he gets your motor running?"

"Better than my favorite book boyfriends and more romantic."

"You're joking?"

I shake my head, feeling better.
"Get up. You're going out."

Chapter Seven

✶ ✶ ✶

Will

"Bring a round in honor of the birthday boy," Josh orders and raises his bottle when the waiter returns.

"Another one? I'm not going to be able to walk tomorrow," Billy protests.

"That's what you get for starting early. You were already four beers in when we picked you up."

"It's Dad's fault. He closed a massive deal today and wanted to celebrate. Plus, it's my birthday."

"Tonight is all about you, buddy." Jackson slaps him on the back. "Whatever you want to do."

"What *do* you want to do?" Josh asks with excited expectation.

"Find a beautiful woman and drink with my best friends until I pass out, preferably in said woman's lap or bed."

"Alright. Will, get to work," Jackson jokes. "Billy's made his birthday wish."

I laugh. Billy and Josh ask for the same thing every year, and carrying out their birthday wishes has been a tradition of ours since freshman year of high school. I can't back out now.

Feeling mischievous, I stand and survey the room. "What can I bring you tonight, my friend? Blonde, brunette, red…" I lose all motor functions when Sydney steps into my line of sight.

After she ran off this afternoon, I didn't expect her to show up. Her tight jeans and light green sweater hug every delicious curve I felt earlier, and I'm struck once again by how beautiful she is. Her long hair is tied up in a high ponytail, my kryptonite, and her lips, the ones I could still taste, are plump and glossy.

"How about a—" Billy begins, but I can't wait for his decision.

"I'll be back."

My heart is pounding as I take a direct path to her. She continues searching through the crowd, a pronounced frown on her pretty face, and that bothers me. Bothers me to think I may be the reason for it. But urgency pushes the thought aside when she shakes her head and turns toward the exit. A few yards away from her, I call out, but the blaring music muffles my voice, and she rushes out the door.

No, no, no.

"Sydney! Wait!" I yell, stepping outside and locating her in the parking lot. She spins around, surprised to see me.

"I shouldn't have come."

"I'm glad you did." Desperate to touch her again, I jog closer and cautiously run my hands down her arms. The last time I saw her, she was determined to walk away. To throw away what we could have. I wonder what changed, but I also don't care. She's here with me now. "Please don't go."

She won't look at me—her eyes stay focused on the ground between us. I drop a kiss to the top of her head and feel her deep inhale. "I want you to stay."

Her shoulders tighten, like I touched a sore spot, before her head lifts. "Why?"

"Why?"

"Why do you like me?" she asks. "Besides the obvious."

"You mean besides you being the most beautiful woman I've ever seen?"

She grins, and I hope that means she's warming to the idea of staying…the idea of us.

"You make me feel something I've never felt before," I continue.

"And what is that?"

"Like I can't breathe without you. Like all that matters now is making you happy."

Her forehead drops to my chest. "It's not fair."

"What's not?"

"You having to leave right after we meet."

I pull her into my arms, wishing for the first time since enlisting that I didn't have to go back. "I know, but it's not forever. If I'm lucky, you'll remember me when I return, and we can pick up where we leave off tomorrow."

"Tomorrow?" she asks, leaning back. It's dark here in this corner of the parking lot, lit only by the faint glow of a few neon signs on the building behind me. But it's enough to highlight the soft contours of her face and the sadness in her eyes.

Then, it's like I was dumped into a frozen lake, my life raft nowhere in sight. I'm the one who clouded the bright emerald of her eyes with sadness. I'm the one who pursued her and convinced her to take the chance. She's scared to get hurt, but that's exactly what I will have to do to her soon. No matter how long I'm gone, it's still going to hurt to be apart. That I'm certain of.

I can't think about that. My only goal for the next twenty-four hours is to make her smile.

"Can I see you tomorrow?"

"I was hoping that's what you meant. You can kiss me now," she says and rises to her toes.

Every sense rams into overdrive when she pulls me down to her, and my mind goes blank. All I can do is let my body react, follow her commands. At the first touch of our lips, hers parted instantly, and I've never wanted anything or anyone more.

But just as I am settling in, she leans back and peers up at me, determination in her cloudy eyes. Thankfully, the storm is brewing for a different reason this time, and that ignites a fire in more places than just my lower half.

"I need to say something before you knock the wind out of me again." Her voice is low and breathy while her eyes stay locked on mine, holding me captive.

"I do that to you, too?"

She smiles, and the world seems to tip off its axis a little, making me dizzy.

"Yes," she confirms.

"Good. Now, what do you want to tell me? Because I'm not sure how much longer I can wait to finish that kiss."

She places a hand on my chest, a silent reminder for me to pay attention. This is important.

"I'm sorry for leaving the way I did earlier," she says, dropping her eyes to the chain draped around my neck. When she doesn't continue, I look down and realize she's holding my dog tags, lost in what they symbolize for us.

"It's okay," I tell her, hoping to set her mind at ease.

"Thank you, but it wasn't fair to you, and you've been so sweet to me." She lets go of the tags and presses them to my chest with her palm. "I haven't had the best luck in the relationship department, and I was afraid to like you."

"How do you feel about me tonight?" I bend to kiss her neck, and she tilts her head, opening for more.

"Overwhelmed. Hopeful," she sighs. "Like I can't breathe without you."

Chapter Eight

✯ ✯ ✯

Sydney

"Wake up!" Nora yells and jumps onto my bed. "There's a delivery for you."

"A what?" I ask, still groggy from a restless night. Several hours ago, I went against everything I convinced myself was best and dove headfirst into a relationship—a soon-to-be long-distance relationship—with someone I barely know. I cover my face with a pillow and groan.

"Hurry up." Nora reaches for my robe and tosses it at me. "Put this on."

"Why? Can't you bring me the package? I'm so tired."

"No. You're getting up and seeing it for yourself." She throws the covers off me, and I shiver from the sudden rush of cold.

"Alright, alright." After slipping on the robe, I let it hang loose as I shuffle after her down the hall to where it opens to the living room. My tired eyes land on a very gorgeous, wide-eyed, and smiling Will Mason sitting on our couch. He makes the full-size couch look like a loveseat, and my gaze takes in all of him, including the small bunch of flowers in his hand and the full grocery bag at his feet.

In standing, his eyes travel up my body, reminding me of what I'm wearing…or not wearing. A skimpy and very thin gray tank top with no bra and the cotton shorts I've been squeezing into since high school.

"Good morning," he says, and the sound of his husky voice kickstarts my brain. I close the robe and tie it around my waist, pinching my lips at the disappointment that crosses over his face.

"What are you doing here?" I ask.

He waits for Nora to slide out of the room almost undetected before answering. "We have a date."

"But not for a couple more hours."

"I couldn't wait." It takes only two steps with his long legs to close the distance between us and circle an arm around my back. Pulling me to him, he presses his lips to mine. Air snags in my lungs as it seems to do every time he touches me. "Couldn't wait to do that either. These are for you."

"You spoil me." I sniff the bright orange and red blossoms but keep my eyes on him. "I'll add these to the others."

"Others?"

I can't tell if he's puzzled or shocked or both.

Sheepish, I look up. "After you left, I rescued the flowers you gave me yesterday from downstairs."

"You kept them?" he asks, sweetness dripping off his words. "Even though…"

"Of course. Just because I denied my feelings, doesn't mean I didn't appreciate the gesture."

He nods. There is nothing else to be said on the matter. "Oh, I also brought breakfast. Well, more like I brought stuff to use in making breakfast."

"You're going to cook?"

"No. *We're* going to cook."

I shake my head, tossing up my hands. "I don't think that's a good idea. We just met. I'm not ready to kill you off yet."

"Excuse me?"

"She can't cook a lick," Nora explains on her way by with her jacket and waitress apron in hand. "Don't mind me. I'm on my way to work, which is where I will be for the next five hours." She winks at me and then smiles at Will.

"Nora!"

"Just sayin'." She opens the door, then stops to lean on the knob. "I'll also knock before entering," she quickly adds as she closes the door, preventing me from scolding her further.

Will chuckles. "She's awesome."

"Seriously, about breakfast," I say, returning to this crazy cooking idea of his. "I don't want to kill you."

"There's no way you're that bad."

I glare down my nose at him.

"Fine. I'll do all the cooking, and you can keep me company." He reaches for the bag on the floor.

"That I can handle. Kitchen's through there," I point to a door behind him. "I'll be right back."

"Where are you going?"

"To change."

"Please don't."

"Why?"

"It's just…" He swallows hard, and I wonder if I am prepared for what he is about to say. The tender way he looks at me and the words he uses have a way of making me come undone. But this time all he says is, "I don't want you to."

And that is more than enough for the untethering to begin. "Okay."

He holds out his hand, and together, we enter the apartment's miniature galley kitchen.

"What did you bring?" I manage through the thick fog of desire that snapped into the air with his touch.

"All the fixings for omelets and…" He reaches into the bag and slowly pulls out a small white box with a gold sticker.

"You didn't."

"I did."

I snatch the box of fudge from his hand and toss open the lid to breathe in the sweet, familiar scent.

"Do you eat anything else?" he asks with a smirk.

"Yes, I eat other things. Fudge just happens to be my favorite."

"Figured that out already, and that's why we're going to learn how to make it tonight."

"We are?" I set down the box when his chest swells and his mischievous smile switches to one of those I'll-ask-for-forgiveness-later types of smiles. He's mastered the look. "Where are we doing this?"

"My mother happens to be an amazing cook, and she's going to give us a lesson."

I freeze while the healthy appetite I had moments ago slinks away. "I'm meeting your mother tonight?"

"And my father. Is that okay?"

"Wow. I mean, yes. I mean…I'm a little surprised, that's all."

He places his hand on mine. "You're not a weekend fling to me, Sydney. What I feel for you already…it's real. I hope you know that."

"I didn't at first. That's why I ran. I was scared you only thought of me as temporary. You know, a weekend fling, as you put it, before going back to your life." I drop my eyes, embarrassed to admit where my thoughts went after our romantic romp in the grass.

"If that were the case, I wouldn't be here with promises on the tip of my tongue. I don't make promises, Sydney. Never."

I can't think, breathe, move. The intensity and honesty in his eyes are both convincing and earth-shattering. "What promises are you talking about?" I manage, but my voice is only a whisper.

"Exclusive ones. I want you to be mine. No matter what happens next week or where we are."

"Okay."

"That's it? You don't need more convincing? Because I came prepared."

"Well, if you want to grovel, I'm willing to change my answer." I cross my arms and hold his gaze. This man, this very beautiful man cooking me breakfast, is asking to be my boyfriend, and he brought fudge…again.

"Nah. I'm good." He winks and cracks an egg into a bowl without looking. "You don't eat fudge in your eggs, do you?"

"Eww."

"Had to check."

"So, what else do you have planned for us today?" I ask to bring my heart back to a normal rhythm, but he's distracted, hunting through the drawers. "Next one."

"Thanks." After grabbing a fork, he begins whisking the eggs. "I thought we'd hang out here until dinner, unless you're interested in an adventure." He waits to see if I react.

"What kind of adventure?"

"Well, my buddy owns a zero-gravity airplane business." He grins. "But if that's not your speed, we can—"

"Is that *your* speed?"

"Actually, it's a little slow for my taste."

"Hmmm." Apparently, my new boyfriend is a daredevil. "How do you feel about scuba diving?"

He shrugs and rips open a package of bacon. "I'd give it a three out of ten."

"Cliff diving?"

"Eight out of ten and one of my favorites."

"Skydiving?"

"Nine."

"Have you done it?"

"Multiple times," he admits casually.

I sigh, trying to figure out how I feel about that little nugget of information.

"The boys and I like to find things to do while on leave."

"Skydiving and cliff diving aren't something you just do. How does a zero-gravity airplane rank in your life-threatening adventures?"

"Around a two."

I lean on the counter as he places the last piece of bacon into the sizzling pan and the sweet maple scent fills the room. "So, you just float around in the back of an airplane? Doesn't sound very exciting."

"That's why I gave it a two. But I have some ideas to improve that number." His trademark naughty smirk appears before he looks away to flip the bacon slices.

"Oh, yeah? I need to know what that is before I agree to this little *adventure*."

Without a word, he slides the pan off the burner, then stands in front of me. His feet straddle mine. All I can do is watch his face. His dark eyes are near black now. Lost in them, I hadn't realized he had untied my robe until his hands circled my waist.

His breath is hot on my neck, and I want to touch him. I want to pull him closer and feel his body against mine. But my muscles have gone lax, and I'm already gripping the counter for support.

"I plan to do more than just float," he whispers next to my ear, then pulls back to meet my gaze.

He's testing me, wondering if I'm going to run, but I couldn't even if I wanted to. Being apart from him is no longer an option. I need him, want him.

"Show me."

He inches closer, his lips hovering over my cheek and then the corner of my mouth. Exactly where I'm craving him to touch, taste, savor. Then, his hands slide up my sides to frame my face, and when I'm dizzy with anticipation, he pushes back.

"Later," he says flatly and returns to the stove.

I'm panting with potent tingling sensations radiating through my veins and stealing my ability to perform simple bodily functions.

"Later?" I manage, and he smiles over his shoulder, obviously proud of himself. Jerk.

"When we're up there." He points the tongs to the ceiling and beyond. "If you knew what was coming, it wouldn't raise that two to a six."

"Only a six, huh? Sounds like you need to up your game."

Chapter Nine

✯ ✯ ✯

Will

We decide to eat breakfast sitting on the floor around the living room coffee table. It's cozier, she explains, and I have to agree. Plus, it's the perfect setting for our next activity.

"What's that?" she asks when I set a game of Jenga on the table.

"Do not tell me you've never played?"

"Of course, I've played. Just wondering why you brought it."

"This is not your normal game of Jenga. It's more…interactive." I carefully remove the group of narrow wooden pieces already neatly stacked together from the box.

She takes a bite of scrambled eggs and closes her eyes. "This tastes amazing," she says and shoves another bite into her mouth.

"Thanks." After sneaking a bite of bacon, I clap my hands together in anticipation. This should be fun. "Each piece has a question on it that you have to answer. If you refuse, the other person gets that block which counts as a point. Whoever has the most points wins or, as usual, if you make the tower fall—"

"Yeah, yeah. Loser. I know."

I laugh. "Let's hope that doesn't happen because I can't wait to hear your answers to some of these."

"This is like speed dating."

"Exactly. And since we have only one day…" I trail off, not thrilled to be saying goodbye to her tomorrow.

"We have only one day to make sure the other isn't crazy and actually worth this foolish dating idea."

I take her hand. "I already know you're worth it. Now, I need to make sure you're not a psychopath."

She yanks her hand away. "Thanks a lot."

"Hey, you said it." She's so cute when she's pretending to be tough. "Go. You're up first." I nod toward the tower.

"Fair warning." She grins and adjusts into fight mode on her knees. "I'm super competitive."

"Good. I am, too. Glad I don't have to worry about you having any sissy reactions."

"No need for those when you win. I don't have to worry about you being a sore loser, do I?" She picks up a slice of bacon and takes a bite.

"Nope, because I never lose."

"There's a first for everything, as you've recently learned." She smirks before taking another bite and chews while confidently removing the first wooden piece. After reading the question written on the side of the block, she slumps back on her heels.

"What's it say?"

"Tell me again. What happens if I don't answer?"

I let out a chuckle. "It's the first block."

"Tell me."

"You lose a point," I answer, confused.

"Damn."

Her heart rate has increased. I can tell by her short, rapid breaths. "Remember why we're doing this?" I ask to soothe her.

"So you can make sure I'm not crazy."

That brings a smile to my face. "No. To get to know each other better. I want to know everything. The good, the bad, and the painful."

"And you'll do the same?"

My hand shoots up in a pledge. "No secrets."

"Okay."

When she continues to stare at the block, struggling to start, I gently pull it from her fingers and read the question: *Why did your last relationship end?*

"I don't know," she answers. "The last time we were together, he insisted we go out to a fancy dinner. He said I deserved it." She rolls her eyes, and they land on her hands in her lap. "But right before the check comes, he leaves. No warning or explanation. I had no car, very little money, and it was late."

"What an ass."

"He had a taller, sexier blonde on his couch when I went to get answers the next day. Needless to say, I swore off your species after that."

She tries to smile, but it won't form, and I seriously consider finding the asshole before I leave.

"I get it, but I hope you know I'm not him."

"Yes. Trevor was a jerk, even before that night. He liked to build me up so he could tear me down. He preferred me under his foot."

"Sydney, I—"

"Don't." Her bravery and determination strike me speechless. "I'm glad it happened. I know the signs to avoid now."

"Do you see any of those in me?"

She holds my gaze, studying me, and sweat begins to bead on my back in the silence. "No," she finally whispers, to my relief, then smiles. "But the game just started, so the jury's still out."

"Alright. Let's hope you find me innocent."

"Highly unlikely. Your turn."

I frown then pick up my fork. "I need some nourishment first. I could pull a doozy like yours." I shove a big bite of the omelet in my mouth and focus on the tower before selecting a target. It glides out without jiggling the rest. "What's your favorite color?" I read aloud.

"Seriously? I get the horrible breakup block and you get your favorite color?"

"It's a game of chance, gorgeous. Deal with it."

She lets out an exaggerated sigh, making me laugh.

"Well? What's your stupid favorite color?" she asks, tossing up her hands in frustration.

"Guess."

She looks me over, touching her finger to her chin. I could have her do that all day. Her eyes have a depth behind them. Like she's lived two lifetimes already and is used to fighting for her happiness. And it hits me: I don't want her to fight anymore. I want to be the source of her happiness.

She snaps me out of my distracting thoughts when she answers. "Red."

"How'd you know?"

"Easy. Most of the flowers you brought me yesterday and today were red or a shade of red. And it was the color of your shirt and the paper flower from the day we met."

"Very observant of you."

"And I have red hair."

"That's why you're my favorite. Next block."

With reluctance, she removes another and reads the question with one eye closed. "Oh, thank God."

"Get a good one?"

"Generic dream job question. I've got three more semesters, and I'll be able to start applying for that job."

"What is it?"

"Guess," she teases.

"English teacher?" She shakes her head and bites her bottom lip. I can't think when she does that. "Ugh, nurse? Veterinarian? Zookeeper? Phlebotomist?"

She laughs. "Zookeeper? Why are you only naming medical or animal-related jobs?" She folds her arms and narrows her eyes at me.

"Well, you took care of Ms. Stanley and Mr. Darcy, and those jobs seemed to fit. The zookeeper one was to make you laugh. I give up."

"Good. That was exhausting. Accountant," she announces proudly, but I don't get it. My expression must have told her so. "What?" she asks.

"Never would have guessed that one."

"Yep." She takes a sip of her juice and smiles over the glass. "In less than a year, I'll be able to do your taxes."

"Exciting."

"Isn't it? Next question."

Still recovering, I yank out a block, forgetting to be careful, and the tower spins and wobbles a little. We gasp in unison and freeze in place until it resettles.

"Way to go, fumble fingers." She points at the block in my hand, and I glance down.

"Nope. You can have the point." I toss it across the table and reclaim my fork. Suddenly, I'm famished and need to consume my omelet all at once.

"What did it ask? How many sex partners you've had?" She laughs until I don't. I'm too busy shoving more bites into my full mouth to join in. "What's the matter? Too many to count?"

"Your turn," I mumble.

"I thought you said there would be no secrets."

Damn it. I did. "I—"

"How about we say our answers at the same time? Then, it's all out in the open for us both."

"Okay," I agree with strong reluctance since dating has never been my speed. I prefer experiences over relationships, especially since I'm never in one place for more than a few weeks. But Sydney makes me want to change that. At least, she makes me want to try to make it work. To be a better person. To commit and fall in love for the first time.

"Ready?" she encourages, but my mouth is dry. My stomach is constricting like I've been crawling through the desert with no food or water for days. I've been there…this is worse. What if my answer makes her bolt or look at me differently?

I hold up a finger and take a sip of her juice. "Alright. I'm ready."

"On the count of three," she instructs, and I nod. My heart is pounding in my ears. What if *her* number is high? I can't even think of her with another man, much less many. Vomit rises into my throat when she starts the count.

"One. Two. Three!"

She holds up four fingers as I say, "I don't know."

Her hand slowly lowers to her lap. Her eyes lock on mine as she tries to decipher what my answer means. "So, you've had more than you can remember. Who were they to you?"

"Sydney."

"Were any of them girlfriends?"

"No."

"I see." She looks out the window and contemplates before returning to me. "Then, you've never dated anyone exclusively?"

"No."

"In that case, how do I know you'll be faithful to me?"

It's a valid question, and she deserves an honest answer. "You don't. But it's not like I can't do it. I've just never wanted to before. I'm always away." Why is this so difficult to explain? I'm only making myself sound like an insensitive cliché. "Sydney, I give you my promise." My heart aches from the fear darkening her eyes.

"What promise?"

"All of them. I want this to work." I shift to my knees, crawl to her side of the table, and pull her into my lap. "I want us to work…more than I've ever wanted anything."

"You barely know me. How can you say that?"

"Because everything feels different with you. I feel whole, inspired, happier, better." I trail a finger across her cheek, hoping she'll look at me. I need to see her eyes, and I pray there's something favorable in them. "How do you feel with me?"

She lifts her eyes then and it breaks me. They're full of tears. "I already told you."

"When?"

"Last night."

"Tell me again."

She turns in my lap to face me squarely, her knees on either side of my hips. Her arms wrap around my neck, but before I can remember to breathe, she kisses me and fills me with life again.

"I don't know why," she begins, pulling back and moving her hands to my chest. "But I want you with me. I can't continue the way I was before. You're a part of me, and I never knew that piece was missing until we met."

I bring her hand to my lips, hoping she knows how much those words mean to me. How much *she* means.

"I don't care how many women you've been with, and I believe you when you say you'll be faithful. Again, I don't know why. Maybe blind or hopeless wishing or—"

"No." My hands frame her face. "You believe me because it's true, and we are meant to be together."

"You're right. I feel it in my soul."

She leans forward and presses against me, and I have nowhere to go but to her lips. Like a magnet, I'm drawn to her and the pull that keeps bringing me back to her. Our bodies melt together, and there's nothing else. No noise from the traffic outside. No apartment or responsibilities or worries about the future.

Just us.

Chapter Ten

✶ ✶ ✶

Sydney

What is it about this man that feels so good? I should stop this. I shouldn't be straddling him, leading this seduction train. It's his fault. When he touches me, I morph into the conductor of a runaway steam engine, and I can't help myself.

"We should keep playing the game," I say to pump the brakes and put some space between us.

"If you want."

He seals the proposed treaty with a slow and meandering kiss along my neck, and I no longer remember what I said. My head tilts, taking it in. I didn't mean to, but my body has taken over this train and is threatening to jump the tracks.

A sigh oozes out of me. "I want a lot of things right now, but the only safe one on the list involves you pulling another block."

His hand moves to my cheek, and I lean against it, committing this moment to memory before opening my eyes—prepared to follow through.

He must recognize my resolve because after a pause, he says, "Okay. But I think it's your turn."

"Really?"

"Yeah. Last question was—"

"Got it. I remember." No need to rehash that one. I reach for a block without shifting off Will's lap. I'm happy right where I am.

We read the question together: *Do you have any siblings?*

"An older brother, Conor," I answer. "He's twenty-five, three years older."

"Same as me."

That makes me smile. "Your age is the only thing you two have in common."

"Yeah? So, he's not a romantic gentleman with irresistible charm and personality?" A wide grin graces his handsome face and sweetness brightens his eyes, bringing the same soft light to mine, but it's fleeting.

"I wouldn't know about that. We haven't spoken in years. He moved back to Ireland."

"How do your parents feel about that?" he asks.

"Out of the two of them, the only opinion that matters is my mother's, and she approves. He can do no wrong. He goes to church, volunteers at the church, is married to an Irish Christian woman, and calls home weekly."

He separates my hands and brings them to his lips when he notices me picking at the chipping hunter-green polish on my nails. "How dare you not call your mom every week."

I laugh. "Do you call your mom that often?"

"No, but I have an excuse."

"You better not be taking her side," I warn, prepared to go to battle over the matter.

"Absolutely not." He holds up his hands in surrender before softly taking mine again. "Seriously. Who cares that you don't go to church?"

"My outlandishly strict, Bible-abiding, old-fashioned mother who thinks I should be married and pregnant by now."

"Whoa! You're twenty-two."

"Yeah. I know."

"Well, thank the Lord that you are the stubborn, strong, and independent woman she disapproves of." He pulls me into his arms and nibbles my shoulder, helping me forget how frustrated I get whenever thoughts of my mother make an appearance. "Otherwise," he continues, "we may not be here together right now. I don't date pregnant chicks."

"That's smart, but I thought you didn't date anyone, expecting or not."

"Good point. Well, you changed that, but I'm still glad you aren't pregnant." He pecks my nose and reaches across me to snatch another block from the tower, making it wobble. "What's the—"

"Wait." I hold a finger to his lips to stop him from reading the rest of the question. "Do *you* have any siblings?"

"Nope. My parents tried, but I was all they could handle." He winks in that flirty up-to-no-good way of his.

"No doubt."

"They wanted a big family, but they had to settle for Billy, Josh and Jackson being their adopted sons."

"I'm sure they didn't see it as settling. All right, read your question."

He holds it up. "What's your most embarrassing moment?"

"Finally. A good one. Spill it." I drape my arms over his shoulders, ready for a juicy confession.

"That's a hard one. I don't embarrass easily."

"Not surprised, but there has to be something you wish didn't happen or you could go back and change."

A laugh escapes his pinched lips as though he had been trying to hold it back and gave up…or lost the struggle.

"What is it?"

He wrangles the laughter into a toothy smile, making my skin shimmer with adoration.

"You're right. One embarrassing moment comes to mind, but I don't want to take it back. It's priceless."

"Tell me," I manage after catching his infectious laughter.

"Three years ago in Miami, I was flirting with some women. One of them was eyeing Billy, so I introduced them, and another to Josh." His hand covers his mouth as more laughter steals his ability to speak. "Soon, their entire group joins us, and we hang out until the bar closes. It isn't until the cab ride back to the hotel that we discover…"

"Discover what?"

"Among the ten of us, there wasn't one woman in the group."

"What?" I ask, confused. But he doesn't continue. Instead, he waits for me to process the information, and when I do, my hand smacks over my mouth. "No way," I mumble from behind my fingers.

"Yep. Every one of them was a dude dressed in drag. It was hilarious to see Billy and Josh's reaction. I'll never forget it." He throws his head back laughing, lost in the memory. "But after they got over their shock, the rest of the night was a blast. We played poker, hung out by the pool, and did typical man shit. Just half of us were wearing skirts or dresses."

"That is funny, but why was that an embarrassing moment for you? Were Billy and Josh not the only ones flirting?" I accuse, and his smile widens.

"Flirting's my thing. I never let an opportunity to use my skill go to waste, especially when my boys ask me to bring them some ladies. So yeah, I was in on it…but only in the beginning."

"Right. I bet you—" But before I can finish that sentence, he tosses the block over his shoulder and shifts to pin me against the floor.

"You bet what?" he asks, the words gliding off his tongue in a low growl.

"I bet…that your charm is lethal for both men and women." I lay a long, lazy kiss on his lips. "Dangerous as predicted."

"Not anymore."

"Hanging up your playboy hat, are you?" My voice is flowing along a sultrier path, and I like how it's making Will squirm. His muscles are tighter now. Another internal battle has commenced inside him, and it's easy to tell which side is losing by the way his gaze locks on mine.

"Tossed out the window exactly…" He lifts my wrist to glance at my watch. "Forty-six hours and thirteen minutes ago."

"Hmmm. Good to know."

His fingers comb their way through my hair, splaying across the shaggy carpet. When he reaches the end, he curls a lock around his forefinger and twists.

"I love your hair," he finally says, unraveling the lock from his finger and starting again. "I have a hard time keeping my hands out of it when we're together."

"You don't have to do that."

"Yes, I do."

My pulse buzzes under my skin from the subtle change in his tone. It was both smooth and ragged. Only Will can pull off that contrast. But the room is silent now, allowing me to focus on his body pressing against mine. My breathing is rusty and shallow. Not from the weight of him or his sexy pine forest scent filling my lungs, but from anticipating the moment his gaze reconnects with mine. I adore the tender way he studies me, like everything about me is intriguing and new. But at the same time, I'm weary that those watchful eyes are going to unravel me.

"I need a shower," I blurt out for a distraction and to avoid having to deal with the consequences of an unrestrained unraveling.

"I'm in."

"Not what I meant," I correct and sit up, rolling him off me. "We should slow down. Not throw coal on the fire with naked wet time."

"God, that sounds amazing." His lips go for my neck in ravenous fashion, and it takes all I have not to let him. "Come on," he complains. "We haven't even finished the game, and I was really liking where it was going."

"What about that adventure you were going to somehow improve from a two to a six?"

"Oh, right. Fine. I'll set it up while you enjoy naked wet time without me." He pouts, his bottom lip poked out, and it's the cutest thing ever.

I peck his nose and pop up. "Don't go anywhere. I won't be long."

"I'll stay right here, thinking about you…naked."

"Ha."

―――

"Shit." When I reach for my towel on the rack, all I grab is emptiness. In a hot frazzled mess, I forgot to grab a towel from the laundry room before jumping in the cold shower.

I look around. There's nothing but a used hand towel on the sink and my silk robe and pajamas. The bathroom sits at the end of the hallway and opens to the living room. I have no choice.

"Hey, Will?" I call, cringing at my bad luck.

"Yeah?"

"Would you mind grabbing me a towel from the dryer? The laundry room is off the kitchen."

"Happily."

I roll my eyes. This mishap isn't helping us slow our pace. Then, Nora's words rattle in my thoughts. *Have fun and enjoy the orgasms.* I shiver, and it isn't from the cold water on my skin. I wonder what all those muscles of his look like under that navy blue T-shirt. It does a great job of showcasing his frame, and his massive biceps peek out from under the sleeves often enough to make me salivate. I wouldn't mind seeing a row of his six—

"Can I come in?" Will's voice is muffled on the other side of the door.

"Yes, but keep your eyes closed." The shower is surrounded by glass. Clear, exposing, see-everything glass.

"Do I have to?"

"Yes."

The door creaks open, and he shuffles in, one hand over his eyes and another holding out the towel.

"No peeking," I demand and cover my woman parts as best I can with my puny arms. I really need to start working out.

"Wouldn't dream of it. Where are you?"

"You can drop it there."

"You must be freezing." He grabs two ends of the towel and opens it, keeping his eyes clenched shut. "Come here."

"No. You're dangerous."

"Come on. Let me warm you up." He smiles. "I promise I won't look."

"You know, you make a lot of promises."

"And I plan to keep every one of them."

I creep out of the shower. "I have no idea why I trust you. You have a very mischievous face." And tempting. But despite that, I tiptoe closer and allow him to wrap me in both the towel and his strong arms. As he rubs my back, I start to relax in his warmth, and we soon begin to sway to silent music.

I could stay like this for days. I feel safe, appreciated, content. Nothing is better than being in his arms. Not even fudge.

He kisses my forehead, then looks down at me. "Ready to get dressed? Our appointment's in an hour."

A meek "Sure" is all I can muster after seeing the tender sweetness in his eyes. Trevor never looked at me like I was precious to him. Never told me he couldn't breathe without knowing I was his. He never held me to provide comfort, and he certainly never made promises. But even if he had, I wouldn't have believed him. Wouldn't have trusted with every fiber of my being that he did so without an ulterior motive or for manipulation. No. Will's promises are different. He makes them only because he believes in us.

With his arm draped over my shoulders, he walks me to my room. And by the time he closes the door behind him, I am hopelessly and completely in love with Will Mason.

"I have to hand it to you, Mason. You've upped your game as challenged," I rave as we sit down to an early dinner at a trendy new bistro in downtown Richmond.

"I take it you enjoyed the flight?"

"I liked your romantic touches the most. I've always wanted to kiss a sexy man while floating."

"Really?"

"No," I laugh, "but had I known that was a thing, it definitely would be top of the bucket list. The rose petals…" I shake my head, remembering.

They were sprinkled on the hangar floor, and when we started floating, they drifted into the empty space around us. It was the most romantic thing I'd ever experienced. That is until he snatched me from the air and held me close, our legs wrapped around each other. We kissed the entire flight, hovering in the petals and heat. Our bodies locked like puzzle pieces meant only for each other. And that, my friend, is the most romantic thing ever.

"There's more where that came from," he boasts, picking up the menu, and all I want to do is find out what else is up that romantic sleeve of his.

"Hmmm," is all I can say, warmth already rising up my neck and into my cheeks. I'm suddenly craving something other than food and it would be best to separate myself from the source of that hunger. "I'm going to run to the restroom. Order me ice water?"

"Sure." A sweet grin graces his lips, and I press a kiss there before leaving the table. That should pacify me enough to get through dinner. Maybe.

How did I get here? Not here physically, but here in love with Will? I'm not even supposed to be talking to those of his gender, but in a matter of two days, I find myself—

"Sydney?"

I whip around at the sound, instantly regretting it. The ladies' restroom is a few feet away. Why couldn't I have stepped inside like I never heard him?

"Hi, Trevor." This is the first time I've seen or spoken with him since our breakup. Correction, since he left me.

"What are you doing here?" His eyes travel down my body, taking in all of me. I had changed clothes after the romantic space float to dress appropriately for dinner and meeting Will's parents. By the appreciative expression on Trevor's angled face and the pop in his jaw, he approves of my polka-dotted summer dress and strappy leather heels. I used to dress like this often to receive that look from him. Now, seeing it makes my skin crawl.

"I was just leaving," I answer curtly and turn back toward the dining room. Being near him is rattling me more than I care to admit.

"Wait. It's wonderful to see you. How have you been?"

"Great. Better than great," I oversell, but fortunately, it is true. My heart is whole, no thanks to him, and I love my life, my freedom, and myself again. "How are your classes going?" I ask, casual and unbothered.

"It's a lot of work, but it will be worth it one day."

Trevor is a pre-med major. His father, grandfather, great-grandfather, and generations before them were doctors, and he's proud to follow in their footsteps. But all that heritage and the expectations and privilege that comes with it have created a self-absorbed, misogynistic, manipulative excuse for a man. I didn't see it until it was too late, and it's even more obvious now that I've been exposed to the exact opposite.

"You look beautiful, Sydney. Who are you here with? Nora?"

I look back over his shoulder, searching for another escape. "I should really get going." I try to step around him, but he adjusts to block my path.

"You're on a date," he infers from my lack of response. "No wonder you're showing so much of your gorgeous legs."

An exasperated sigh oozes out before I can stop it. "Have a nice—"

He snatches my arm as I take another step forward, flaring my aggravation into full-on fury. Who does he think he is?

"I remember when you wore this dress for me," he says in a low husky tone. "And how it looked on you in the morning light as you snuck out of my dorm room."

His thumb glides over my skin as if he has a right to be there. Then, I feel his dark blue eyes travel down to my chest and nausea rises into my throat. Determined not to let him get to me, I push it back down and turn to meet his heated glare.

"How's Billie?" I ask, referring to the platinum-blonde model slash nursing student he left me for.

"It's Millie, and she's fine."

"How do you think she'll feel about you touching your ex-girlfriend in a dark, secluded hallway?"

He doesn't flinch—no surprise there. Instead, he leans in, his breath hot on my cheek.

"I know you think about me, Sydney."

"You're wrong." I turn to face him, determined to prove that I've moved on. That I'm a different person than the one he manipulated and mistreated. Stronger. Capable of protecting myself. "You're the last person I think about. In fact, you never cross my mind. Now, let me go or I'll scream."

His fingers tighten around my arm. "No need for that, Sydney. We're just having a nice talk."

I suck in some courage with a breath. "What's this about, Trevor? You've never been physical." Mouthy and devious but never aggressive.

"This is nothing. Millie likes it rough, and I seem to have a knack for it."

"Then go be with her. We've been long over."

"Don't lie, Sydney. The look in your eyes and your rapid pulse says I still affect you."

"That's because I don't want to be here. Let me go." I yank my arm free and hold his gaze and my ground.

"Fine," he says, stepping back. "But I think I'll stop by your place soon so we can continue this. It's been such a pleasure…reconnecting with you."

Dumbfounded, I stare at him. In what universe did he think I'd want him to stop by? Want *him*?

His eyes start to travel over me again, but I close the distance, making sure I have all his attention. "Don't bother, Trevor. Where you're concerned, that door and every door will stay closed and deadbolted."

And then I walk away, no looking back.

Chapter Eleven

Will

Something's off. When Sydney returned to the table, she was distant, distracted and although she tried to hide it, flustered. She didn't want to talk about what had upset her. All I could do was try to lift her spirits and keep the conversation light and flowing. A few times, she glanced through the restaurant but just as I was about to ask her what was wrong, she refocused me.

"I'm excited to meet your parents," she says after a server removes our empty plates from the table.

"You're not nervous anymore?"

"Well, a little. But after what you've told me, they seem like the sweetest and most loving people. I have a feeling I'm going to fall for them hard."

"Like you have me?" I ask, testing. She's been looking at me differently since we left her apartment, and I've been wondering what changed.

Her jaw goes lax before she forces it closed with a sly grin. "What makes you think I've fallen for you, Mason? I've known you for less than seventy-two hours."

"Yet…"

"Yet…you are pretty irresistible."

"I know."

She laughs, and I'm suddenly tired of having this table between us. "Ready to get out of here?" I ask.

"Let's do it. That sweet dessert you promised is calling my name."

We rise in sync, and I take her hand. But instead of leading her out, I pull her close and lower my lips to hers.

"I was talking about the fudge," she says when I draw back, her eyes remaining closed.

"Oh. I thought you meant me."

Her lashes gradually slide up, and she grins. "Not this time, but I'm expecting to be served all the helpings I want later."

"Now you're talking." I peck her lips one more time, then head toward the exit. But when I open the door, her grip on my hand tightens, and she uses my body as a shield. She should never have to hide, and the fact that she suddenly does bothers me.

I stop when we reach the sidewalk. "What is it?"

"Nothing. Keep going."

"No. I want to know what's making you uneasy. I want to help."

"You can't. Unless you can take me away from here." She looks up at me with desperation. Then, her nervous eyes cut to the man standing to my right.

With his hands in the pockets of his starched white shorts, he's eyeing Sydney as though she's his next meal. That alone is enough to send me off the deep end, but seeing how he makes her uncomfortable, I suddenly understand.

"That's your ex, isn't it?"

Her gaze snaps to mine. "Will, please. We should go."

"Did he do something earlier? Is he why you were so distracted?"

She doesn't answer, but her breath hitches in her chest.

"What did he do? Sydney." I gently take hold of her arms and lower to see her eyes better. They tell me all I need to know without her saying a word.

She shakes her head. "I can handle him."

"But you don't have to anymore."

Her eyes soften when she touches my cheek. Whatever this asshole did to hurt her, I have to make sure it doesn't happen again. For her safety and my sanity.

"When I went to the restroom earlier, I never made it there. He intercepted me and…" Her eyes glisten with fresh tears.

"And what, Sydney?"

"He grabbed my arm and said he would come by my apartment soon."

We're outside near a crowd of people and a busy street, but I can only hear my rage pounding in my ears. I want to retaliate. Teach this jerk a lesson he won't soon forget, but instead, I ask her, "Do you want that? Do you want to see him?" It's like a dagger through the gut, but what she wants matters. "Want him?"

Her brow pinches in the center and her eyes instantly dry. "No! Will." She's shaking her head and clutching my hands in a panic to make me understand. "I only want you."

That makes me smile, and I kiss her forehead. "Good. Then, I'll be right back."

I step toward the asshole as Sydney reaches for me, but I slide free.

"Trevor, is it?" I ask unnecessarily. I already know his name and his type. The guys and I have dealt with scum like him more times than I can count while traveling. Doesn't matter where you are or what language you speak. An asshole is an asshole, and I can spot them a mile away.

"Yeah. Who are you?"

His dismissive tone has my hands balling into fists. "Sydney's boyfriend," I'm happy to answer. Wow. Boyfriend. That's a first, but it has a nice ring to it.

"Oh, really?"

Trevor looks me over, sizing me up, no doubt. Then, the corner of his mouth turns up. Guess he figures he can take me, and I would love to see him try. It's been a while since

I've been in a good bar fight, but I don't foresee this skinny jerk putting up a challenge.

"Since when did Syd start dating again?" he asks.

Syd? That nickname she mentioned, no doubt. "That's none of your concern, and neither is she. You will not talk to her, text her, stop by her apartment, or go near her ever again. She has no interest in seeing you."

"Interesting. So, are you her messenger, or are you controlling her life now?"

"She's fully capable of making her own decisions, and I know what you did." I step closer. At least five inches taller, I have an imposing angle over him. "And it won't happen again."

He straightens and gains only an inch as he faces me. "I don't know who you think you are…"

"I don't *think* I'm anyone. I know. Like I know your dirty hands will never touch her again."

"What if I have no interest in complying with your ridiculous and inappropriate rules? I have a few things I'd like to show—"

My fist smashing against his jaw is a satisfying and unexpected period to that sentence. I shouldn't have done it, but thinking about him terrorizing Sydney while I'm not around to protect her had me seeing red. He needed to be taught a lesson, and the only one that came to mind involved my knuckles connecting with his face.

His knees buckle as Sydney rushes to my side. Disappointment sets in when she pushes me toward my car before I have the satisfaction of seeing his stuttering reaction.

"I won't apologize," I say as she buckles into the passenger seat and looks out the back window. "I didn't care for the guy, and he wasn't conforming to the deal. He will—"

"What deal?" She settles back and stares at me as I put the car in motion.

"That he will never touch you again."

"Or what?"

"What?" Why isn't she happy about this?

"He doesn't touch me or what? What are you going to do while you're at the base or someplace else?"

"He didn't need threats." I smile and turn toward my parents' house. "Ready to make some fudge?"

"Don't go changing the subject, Mason. You might not have solved anything. You might have only increased the stakes."

"I picked up marshmallows, walnuts, and pretzels. I didn't know what you preferred in your fudge, so I got—"

"Will!"

"What? He won't be bothering you anymore. Mission accomplished. He doesn't know I won't be here, and he's a coward."

"You're crazy."

"Never heard that before," I respond sarcastically. According to my mother, crazy might as well be my middle name. With a wink over my shoulder, I take her hand and the last turn. "We're here."

"Crap." She begins to rock in her seat and rub her free hand on her thigh. "You didn't tell me they lived so close to the restaurant."

"It'll be okay. They're going to love you." *As I'm starting to*, I think all too effortlessly. "Come here." I place a finger under her chin and lean closer. She meets me the rest of the way and her warm lips on mine make that 'starting to' flip the switch to 'already there'.

At that revelation, I force myself to separate from her. There's time to think about how that changes literally everything later.

"Ready?" I manage, holding her gaze while trailing a thumb across her soft cheek.

Her shoulders relax. "I'm starting to realize that I'm ready to do anything so long as you're with me."

"Good. Let's go."

"Oh, God."

Chapter Twelve

★ ★ ★

Sydney

"We're in the kitchen, dear," Will's mother yells from inside as we step through the front door. Instinctively, I squeeze his hand, and he raises it to his lips.

"Don't be nervous," he instructs, but my stomach starts doing back-flips when the kitchen comes into view. After smiling down at me, he directs his attention forward. "Hi, Mom."

He crosses the room to her. A tall thin woman with shoulder-length hair the same sandy color as Will's wipes her hands on a towel before giving him a quick hug. Then, her eyes land on me over his shoulder.

"Sydney." She releases her son and looks me over. "Will's description of you and your beautiful red hair did *not* do you justice." She chuckles then wraps me in a hug, longer and tighter than Will's, and I feel more at home than I ever have at my own. My mother doesn't care for public displays of affection, unless scrutinizing eyes and passive-aggressive judgmental comments count.

"Thank you," I manage when she releases me, touched beyond measure.

"I'm Caroline." She glances over at Will who is unloading the bags of ingredients we brought.

"So, you two want to make some fudge?"

"It's her favorite meal," Will jokes and flashes me a wink.

"Well, don't blame you there." She hooks her arm around mine and leads me through the kitchen. "How about a glass of wine before we get started?"

"I'd love some." I look back over my shoulder at Will. He's sporting the widest smile, and the nervous flipping in my stomach leaps into my heart when he blows me a kiss. I wasn't prepared for him and what he brings to my life. How can I feel this way already? He makes me second-guess everything I ever believed about relationships, soul mates, and even my capacity to love.

"Grab a few glasses and your father," Caroline calls to Will, interrupting my downward spiral, and I'm grateful. I'm not prepared to think about what all that means either. "And join us in the dining room."

"Yes, ma'am."

Their house is small but well cared for. Every piece of furniture, items on shelves, and pictures on walls seem to have been passed down through the generations, giving the home a close-knit family feel.

On the way to the dining room, we pass a row of family pictures lining the walls down the hallway. They're like a timeline featuring Will as a baby, child, and teenager, and I long to stop. I want to study and appreciate them, get to know him better through his history, but Caroline continues on.

"Before the guys get here and ruin our girl talk, I have to ask." She smiles sheepishly and takes my hand as we sit together at the small table. "What did you do with my son?"

She laughs, and though I join in, I'm also trying to decipher what she means. "I'm not quite sure. This is the only Will I know."

"Oh, I love your accent. Where are you from?"

"Ireland."

"Lovely." She taps the top of my hand and sits back. "This is so exciting. I've never met any of his female…acquaintances, not even his prom dates." Her eyes widen with her smile, and the look reminds me of Will when he's up to no good.

"This must seem really weird and out of the blue, then," I empathize, feeling the nervous flutters threatening.

"Yeah. It's a little weird but in a good way. I can see why he's taken with you."

"You can?"

"Yes, but it helps that he's already told me what's happened over the last two days." She taps the top of my hand as she sits back. "I want you to know that Will never says anything he doesn't mean. He's as true and loyal as they come. He's a good man," she adds proudly.

"He is, and that's why I've fallen for him." Did I just say that? I haven't even told Will yet but talking with Caroline is like what I've always envisioned a perfect mother-daughter relationship to be. Easy. A safe place to talk about our deepest desires, fears, and dreams without judgment or criticism. We'd know everything about each other and support one another through life's ups and downs. I'm ready to tell Caroline all I've never been able to tell my own mother. "I'm terrified to lose him tomorrow."

"Oh, honey. Don't be. You hold his heart, that's easy to see, and he'll be back. I hope you can be patient."

"I don't really have an option at this point."

"That's sweet. Well, I know we're going to be great friends," she says and places a hand on my arm. "I can't wait for my husband to lay eyes on you. After he got over the shock"—she lets out a giggle—"he was so thrilled to hear that Will—" She stops as Will and his father enter the dining room.

"There she is," the older male Mason says, setting down two glasses and a bottle of wine on the table. "Come here." He waves at me to stand, then reaches out both arms.

"He's a hugger," Will explains as I tentatively rise.

"I'm so happy to meet you."

I step into his long arms, and they swallow me. He's as tall as Will but thinner, and I melt into him, trying to remember the last time I felt this loved. Other than my time with Will, nothing comes to mind.

Will and his mother are talking behind me, but their words don't connect. All I can think about and hold on to is how these people have instantly become my family and how I don't want to let go.

"Jonathan, release that girl. You're probably freaking her out," Caroline protests.

"Right." He draws back, but the warmth of his love and acceptance still cover me, and the peace I'd felt with Caroline continues to grow. "Sorry, dear," he says, his arm still draped around my shoulders. "I've always wanted a daughter."

"It's okay."

Jonathan motions to my chair as he takes the one on the opposite side of the table. Will sits on the end beside me.

"Are you from Richmond?" Jonathan asks, then removes the cork from the wine bottle.

"Sort of. My family moved here when I was ten."

"From Ireland," Caroline chimes in.

"Yes. Dublin. I was such an awkward anomaly at my first American school."

"I doubt that," Caroline soothes. "I bet you held your own as you did when you turned down this handsome fella." She tosses a thumb and smirks adoringly at Will.

An unrestrained laugh bubbles out of me when Will narrows his eyes at his mother in protest, and I'm grateful it wasn't one of my unpredictable snorts. But even if it had been, I wouldn't care. I feel accepted here, snorts and faults included.

"Well," I begin, glancing over at Will. "He took advantage of my weaknesses, and I caved."

"Fudge?" she asks.

"Yes, and he softened me further with unwavering sweetness and compassion."

"That's my boy," Jonathan chimes in. "Gets it from his father."

For the next hour, we talk about school, work, our childhoods, and normal family small talk as though this isn't the first time we've come together. I'm feeling tipsy, but not from the second glass of wine I drained, but from pure uninhibited happiness.

"On that note," Caroline interrupts with a playful and exaggerated eye roll after Jonathan's newest joke falls flat, "bring your wine glasses to the kitchen, and we'll get started on that fudge-making lesson. I'm sure you two are anxious to get back to your alone time."

"She's always been the smartest lady I know," Will says, standing and reaching for my hand. Then, he leans closer and whispers, "And afterward, we can make some other things at your place."

"Thank you, Caroline," I say after accepting another hug.

Will is talking with his father while holding our two pans of fudge with strict instructions to let it sit for the next several hours before eating.

"I'm so glad he's found you," she says, her hands resting softly on my arms. "You're special to him, and now you're special to us."

Tears fill my eyes, and Caroline wipes the one that rolls down my cheek. "I've never felt this welcomed anywhere."

"Good. If you need anything, please text or call or stop by anytime. We'd love to see you."

"I can't tell you how much that means to me."

She hugs me one last time and steps back. "Let's do dinner soon."

"I'd love to…so long as I don't have to cook it."

We laugh, but when Will's hand falls on my back, tingles radiate over my skin, silencing my amusement.

"Ready?" he asks.

I look up, meeting that gorgeous face of his. "Always."

Chapter Thirteen

✯ ✯ ✯

Will

"I have something for you," I say after we resettle on Sydney's couch, the Jenga game still perched on the coffee table.

She tucks her legs under her and faces me with those remarkable eyes that manage to be both adorable and sexy at the same time. "You do?"

I reach into my back pocket and pull out a delicate silver bracelet, the heart pendant dangling from the bottom. "This was my grandmother's. She left it to me because I gave it to her during my senior year in high school. She wore it every day."

"Will." Her hands spring to her mouth. "I can't accept that."

"I want you to have it. It would make me happy to see it on you instead of in a box in my drawer." Well, that was harder than I expected it to be. I gulp down how much I miss my grandmother. How much I know I'm going to miss Sydney over the coming months.

Tentatively, she reaches out her hand, and I secure the clasp around her wrist. After adjusting the chain, I bring the inside of her wrist to my lips and linger there with words of love on the tip of my tongue.

I don't want to leave her. Don't want to give more years to the Marines or take another tour. I don't want to go home tonight or leave for the base tomorrow with no guarantees of when I'll see her again.

My lips trail up the inside of her forearm, and I can feel her pulse. Her heart is pumping as hard and fast as mine. These intimate moments will never get old. Focused on exploring her exposed skin, hoping to find her lips soon, I ignore my cell phone when it vibrates in my pocket. Resting her arm on my shoulder, I trail my hand higher and up her neck.

"Will," she sighs.

A battle rages inside me, and her breathy plea tilts the scales toward the danger zone.

My phone vibrates again, but it barely reaches my overloaded brain. Whenever I'm touching her, every inch of me lights up like a carnival ride traveling at full speed. My thoughts blur. The sounds, colors, and activity of the world around us blend together, making me dizzy. All I can do is hold on and enjoy the rush. It's better than stepping off the highest cliff and falling into the cold, dark water below.

Sydney is my new favorite adventure.

"Will, shouldn't you check that?" she whispers. Her head leans to the side, allowing my fingers to travel across the soft space above her collarbone.

The lights seem to dim and flicker when she turns to press her lips to my palm. That one small gesture of affirmation consumes me and carries me under like a rip tide. But when another two texts announce their arrival, ruining the moment, several choice words slip out.

Yanking the phone out of my pocket, I check the messages. All are from Jackson and Billy, telling me that they're going out and to meet them there.

"Anything important?" she asks.

"No. Just the guys." Without replying back, I turn off the phone and toss it onto the nearby chair.

"Do you have somewhere to be tonight?"

"Absolutely, not. I'm where I'm supposed to be." Forever.

"Good." She takes my hand. "Should we finish our game? You haven't divulged all your secrets yet."

I had other ideas, but a little more brake pumping is probably a better plan. "Shocking that they didn't all come out tonight during our cooking lesson."

"Your parents are so kind. I'm sure they didn't want to embarrass you."

"Because they love you and want to make sure you stick around." I smirk, but I'm not joking.

"I adore them. Almost as much as I do you." She leans forward and waits for a kiss, which I'm happy to provide. "I can't believe how quickly they accepted me. I've never felt that before. Not even with my own family. It doesn't feel real." Doubt flashes in her eyes before she looks down at our hands laced together in her lap.

"Sydney." Patiently, I wait for her to gather the strength to meet my gaze. I need her to understand. Need her to believe in what she's experiencing. To believe in us as I do. "Every second, every feeling, every word is unquestionably real."

"I feel it. It's just sometimes hard to accept. I'm too used to being disappointed."

"We're meant to be together, Sydney. I've never been more certain of anything in my life."

Holding her gaze, I want nothing more than to kiss her until the sun comes up. But she wants to take things slow, and I'm going to honor that—no matter how much it tortures me. "Your turn."

"What?"

"Your turn to pull a block and answer the question."

I smile when she continues to stare at me blankly. If I didn't know better, I'd say she was second-guessing that brake-pumping idea.

"Right."

Swinging her legs off the couch, she slides to the floor, her back against the couch.

I follow her lead, sitting beside her—my new favorite place to be. After I'm settled with my legs stretched under the table, she pulls out a block and confidently reads the question.

"Favorite vacation." She smiles. "That's easy. Anywhere there's a beach."

"Nice."

"What about you?" she asks me.

"Well, we do a lot of traveling whenever we're on leave. Over the last seven-plus years, we've visited about twenty countries and explored the entire east coast since high school."

"But which is your favorite?"

"I guess I've never really thought about it. We're usually just looking for a new thrill. Doesn't really matter where we find it. But if I had to pick a favorite…" I think back over the many places we've explored. I've been everywhere from Thailand to South America to the Netherlands, and my thoughts keep jumping back to one place. We rarely visit any area twice because new experiences are preferred, but this one is the exception. "I swear I'm not sucking up. We went there last year and had so much fun that we often talk about going back."

"Don't tell me Ireland is your favorite."

My answer is a guilty cringe.

"Meant to be, huh?"

"I've been known to say that once or twice." I steal a quick kiss before refocusing on the tower.

My block asks: *What would your first/next tattoo be?*

Sydney leans closer to read with me. "Do you have one already?"

"No. Do you?"

"One. Here." She points to her chest, above her heart.

"What is it?"

"You know I have an older brother." I nod when she pauses. "But I didn't tell you that I also had a little sister. She passed away from cancer—brain tumor—when she was six. Her illness was why we moved here. My parents thought she would get better care in America. She didn't make it out of her fourth surgery."

"That's terrible. I'm so sorry." I take her hand to comfort her.

"The tattoo is her name, Arely, written in Gaelic." She takes a deep breath, then raises her eyes to mine before I can respond. "I don't want to play anymore."

"Okay. What do you want to do?"

"I want you to hold me until morning. To forget about losses and goodbyes. I want to be connected to you for as long as possible. Make love to me, Will."

Her eyes go hazy with desire as she brings my hand to her chest.

"Sydney, nothing would make me happier, and I've thought of that moment more times than I can count. But what about going slow?"

"I don't care about that right now."

"Will you care tomorrow? Will you wish we had waited?"

"I'm not sure."

"Then, let's just be together tonight. Nothing else matters." Kissing her forehead, I pull her close.

Tomorrow is going to kill me.

Chapter Fourteen

✯ ✯ ✯

Sydney

When my alarm sounds, reminding me of my responsibilities, I can think of nothing else but my aching heart. My empty bed. My hollow soul. Since Will left over an hour ago, I've soaked my pillow and an entire box of tissues with a river of tears. It's not fair. He should be here with me.

I glance over at the flowers he gave me. They're beginning to wilt. I should press a few into my journal, but how can I when I can't get out of bed? It hurts too much.

"Sydney? You okay?" Nora asks, peeking into my room. When she spots me still in bed, she steps inside and sits on the end of the bed. "I was in the living room when Will left. He looked…like you do."

Crawling closer, she lies down next to me.

"Talk to me."

I shake my head, unable to do anything but cry out my frustration, disappointment, and fear.

"Would it help if I told you he left a letter?" she says gently. "We talked a bit. He had a hard time walking out. Kept turning around, then talking himself out of it. I thought he was going to wear out the carpet." She chuckles, then frowns. "It was both heartbreaking and beautiful at the same time. He's got it bad, Sydney."

I sniff. "Me, too."

"Have you told him?"

"Not like you mean. He knows I care and want to be with him. That I'll be here waiting."

She checks the clock on my bedside table. "Why don't you read his letter? Maybe it will make you feel better. There's plenty of time before class. Here." She pulls the letter from her back pocket and sets it on the bed. "I'll give you some privacy."

I don't move as Nora rolls off the bed and shuffles out. I stare at the folded notebook paper sitting where Will once had lain. For hours, he held me there while we talked and laughed. I'll never forget how the outside world was forgotten, and there was only us. I've never been happier or more hopeful.

Unfortunately, those blissful feelings left when he did. But maybe Nora is right. Maybe reading his words written with ink to be kept forever will fill me with those feelings again and drag me out of this bed. He wouldn't want me wallowing. In fact, we talked specifically about neither of us allowing that. We had things to accomplish, lives to live. Then, when we're together again, we'll be more prepared to start our future together.

It's not that simple, but it's enough to dry the tears. Reaching for the letter, I hold my breath and unfold it.

―――

My Sweetest Sydney,

Another promise I can make to you is many more of these. As many as I am able to send so I can stay connected with you. But in between letters, please know that you will be on my mind every second we're apart. You have stolen my heart, and I am forever yours.

This weekend was amazing. Meeting you changed my life. Changed me. I've gone from thinking only about myself to thinking about tomorrow and the many years after with you. I hope the near future allows for more time together and you can come visit me at the base like we talked about.

But mostly, I'll be thinking about our time past a weekend here or there. A future where we conquer daily life together and end each day like last night — in each other's arms. Holding you will always be my favorite thing to do.

I hope you will think of me and remember this journey we've started is worth taking. Worth the wait. If we're allowed leave before we deploy, straight into your arms is where I will run.

Yours Forever,
Will

I read his sweet words two more times, and by the end, I am ready to do as he expects. To continue on as I always have. To endure the wait until we can be together again.

Feeling better, I get dressed and hurry across the street to catch the bus. It was difficult to concentrate during class, but I made it through and got to work without shedding a single tear. That is until a bouquet of red, pink, and yellow roses arrived as the bank manager locked the doors.

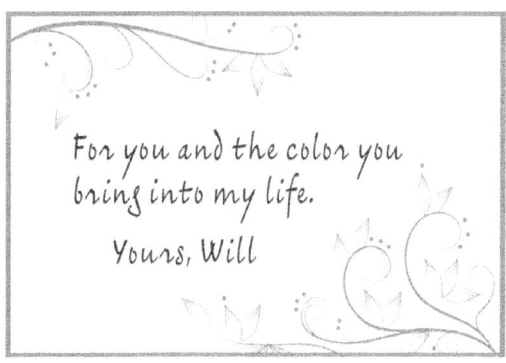

For you and the color you bring into my life.
Yours, Will

"Ugh. Why can't I find a Marine like that? Or a soldier, officer, pilot, anyone? I'm not picky," Denise complains as she sneaks a peek at the card over my shoulder. "They're so beautiful."

I'm barely listening while I reread the card and press my nose to the blossoms. They're perfect, like our love story.

"Is he running in the Marine Corps half marathon next week?" she asks before snatching her timecard off the wall and inserting it in the clock with a loud clank of the stamp.

"What?"

"Your gorgeous, athletic, romantic Marine. Is he running in the marathon next week in Fredericksburg?"

"I don't know," I manage. "He didn't mention it."

"Maybe you should find out. It's only an hour away, and you'll be able to thank him in person for the flowers." She winks, pulling on her backpack and sauntering out.

"Thanks for the tip," I call after her, loving the idea.

"Don't thank me," she begins, poking her head out from behind the door to the breakroom. "Take me with you."

"Maybe I will."

"Alrighty, then."

That evening, Nora and I look up the event online while eating take-out Chinese food from the restaurant beside our complex. The half marathon is happening in just over two weeks. A text from Caroline confirms that Will enters the race with Jackson whenever they are stationed nearby. She even provides some tips on where to park and stay.

That launches another search, and after Nora goes to bed, I spend the next hour researching the visitation requirements for Quantico. At midnight, I finally pass out in bed with my laptop and phone for companionship. It's not the same as a strong, handsome man, but it's all I have until I can see Will again.

It's still dark outside the next morning when a text arrives, startling me out of my dreams. I groan at the loss of the blissful walk I was taking with Will on the beach and snatch my phone off the other pillow.

Who would be texting me at this—

Will: I miss you.

I sit up to respond, but my trembling fingers make it difficult to type. I hadn't expected to hear from him today.

Sydney: I miss you, too. Thank you for the letter. How old-fashioned of you.

Sydney: And incredibly sweet and romantic.

Will: I try. What are you doing today?

Sydney: Got three classes and need to finish a paper. Semester ends in a few weeks. I'll be spending some time at your favorite place.

Will: The bar?

Sydney: Ha! Maybe after I turn in my paper. I was referring to the library.

Will: Hm. Can't say I've ever spent time there, but I do appreciate how it brought us together.

Sydney: There you go being all romantic again.

Will: You kind of do that to me.

Sydney: What are you doing this week?

Will: The usual. Sgt. Jackson keeps us busy with training. Lots to be done to get ready.

Sydney: Have a date yet?

Will: Not yet, but there's talk about early November.

Sydney: That's not too bad. I hate that you'll miss the holidays.

Will: Used to it.

Sydney: Maybe I can come visit you soon to make up for it. I submitted the visitor approval request last night.

Silence.

I stare at the screen for nineteen minutes and thirty-three seconds before giving up and jumping in the shower. It would have been nice to continue our conversation, but he must have been interrupted. At dinner the other night, he described his strict and non-private living conditions with the squad.

He has three roommates, two of which are his best friends, Billy and Josh. Jackson, he said, lives alone since he's the squad's sergeant. Their phone use is very limited, so I remind myself to be grateful for the few texts he was able to send this morning.

I'm trying to stay positive.

———

Sydney's Journal

May 13th

It's been almost a month since I last saw Will. He texts when he can and even called once. He couldn't talk long, and I was at work, but I'll take what I can get.

The letters he sends are so sweet. He could just email me, which he does every now and then, but he says a handwritten letter feels more intimate. It's like we're together when we can hold the paper and feel the indentations of the pen. It's more personal and romantic, he says. And he's right. I swoon over every word on the page more than the emails or texts. There's something to be said for the care and attention it takes to write a letter. It just means more.

In his last letter, he mentioned that he'd been approved as my sponsor. Apparently, my base visit will be easier this way. Now, we need to set a date. My last final for this semester is on Friday, so I'll have more time to take a trip to Northern Virginia.

I still need to fix my car. I should just ask Da to look at it. Who am I kidding? I'd rather walk to Quantico than ask my parents for help. Nora might let me borrow her car if she's not using it. Or maybe Denise would like to go. She could hang out around the base and maybe harass a few Marines at the local bars while I'm with Will.

That should be an easy sell, especially if our trip to the half-marathon goes well next week. Nora's going with us to the race. It's a girls' weekend away to celebrate the end of another year of college. But I hope to see very little of them while in Fredericksburg.

Seeing, touching, kissing, and being with Will is my only focus. He's my reason for going, and thankfully, the girls are the best friends ever. They understand and have made it their mission to help me surprise him.

He's mentioned the half-marathon a few times and invited me to meet him there. In my replies, I told him I was unavailable that weekend and that I'd come to see him at the base soon. I lied, of course.

I can't wait to see the look on his face.

Chapter Fifteen

✦ ✦ ✦

Will

"Try not to choke on my dust," Jackson jokes as he stretches in the shade near the starting line.

"I would say the same to you, but I already know you're going to win the damn race." I continue my regular routine, bending over to loosen my hamstrings. "So, I'll save my breath for the run."

"Good idea." He grins at me before adjusting to the other leg. "You still want to go to the brewery across from the hotel afterward?"

"If I can walk." I'd prefer to sneak away to Richmond for the night to see Sydney, but she mentioned having plans this weekend. To say I was disappointed is an understatement. "Gotta keep up the tradition, don't we? I torture myself for over two hours while you win without breaking a sweat. Then, you pay for all the beers I'm going to drink to forget this shit ever happened."

"Sounds like fun."

"Shut up."

"What's up with you?" Jackson asks before starting his upper body stretches. "You're usually a little more excited than this. Especially about the after-party. We have a free weekend. Let's make the best of it."

"I am. I'm looking forward to getting drunk and having some fun. But the lungs catching-on-fire part leaves a little to be desired."

He laughs, and I straighten to look around. Jackson's right. This weekend usually energizes me. Women, booze, a break from the base. But now, if it doesn't involve Sydney, I don't want to do it.

And I'm upset. Upset she didn't drop her plans for me. It's not like we get a lot of these opportunities. And because I'm letting it get to me, I feel stupid. She has a life outside of our relationship. I can't expect her to always accommodate my unpredictable schedule. But it's not like this marathon was a surprise. I'd mentioned it at least three times. That doesn't make me selfish, does it? I just miss her.

My chest tightens, and I realize I'm acting like a heartbroken teenager. We're both busy adults with established routines and lives before we met. So, from this moment on, I vow to have a good time with my best friend and maybe Sydney will text or call me while she's out with hers.

Damn, I'm pathetic.

"Ready to line up, Corporal?" Jackson asks.

"If you command it, sir."

He rolls his eyes. "Let's go."

"Yes, sir."

———

Eight miles in, and I've lost sight of Jackson. My lungs are on fire as predicted, my muscles ache, and I've thought about quitting more times than I care to admit. It's not like me. I never quit. But my heart's not in it.

Scanning the path ahead, I attempt to get my breathing back on track until I see a water station. Usually I'd breeze past it, snatching a bottle off the table without losing my stride. But this time, I stop. A break to regroup might do me some good.

"Hi, there," the volunteer greets as I stumble to a stop beside her station. She has soft features, powder-perfect skin, blonde hair, and a pronounced southern accent that I immediately recognize as South Carolinian. Normally, my type. "Thirsty?" she asks and bats her long eyelashes.

"Very." I accept the water bottle she offers without another glance and drain half of it.

"Don't drink too fast or you might get a cramp," she says, but her voice sounds different. Less twangy and…familiar.

I yank the bottle from my lips and meet her gaze. She's smiling at me. "What did you say?"

"I didn't say anythang, sweetie."

"Oh." Maybe stopping wasn't the right idea. I hand her the bottle. "Thanks for the drink."

"Anytime."

I take off faster than before to make up for the loss of time and reclaim my sanity. I could have sworn I heard Sydney's voice and the unmistakable Irish inflections she adds to various syllables. I'd know that voice anywhere. It's been haunting me for the last several weeks, in a good way, of course. Except today.

Today, I hear her voice as though she's here. It's wishful thinking and complete torture.

Another mile down, and I'm feeling better. The finish line is closer, I'm still upright, and I've had time to convince myself—again—that I can have fun this weekend. It would be a lot easier if I could confess everything to Jackson. He's my closest friend. I should be able to talk to him about Sydney, but every time I try, I chicken out.

He's sure to have questions tonight when I'm not flirting. I always flirt with women. It's sort of my thing. I've perfected the art and enjoyed the game. But that's not who I am anymore. My heart has been claimed and once again, if it's not with Sydney, I've lost interest.

While keeping pace with the runner in front of me, I watch the spectators. It helps to pass the time to pick faces out of the crowd and create their fictional backstories. Why are they here? Are they simply patriotic, there to support someone running, or hopeful to meet a potential mate? Those are always fun to find. Their stories flow more freely in my mind and keep my thoughts off my burning body.

I've met a few beautiful women in my day through this process. Can't remember any of their names, only the experiences I had with them. Moments here or there. Seven years of marathons means a lot of faces to scan and names to remember. Plus, the information is useless to keep if you never plan on seeing them again. Funny how things can change.

When you meet *the one*. I never thought that one perfect person was out there for me. I've met too many women and felt nothing—well, nothing outside of the intoxicating benefits of sex—to believe it could ever happen. I'm not ashamed to admit that I had been darting around the globe with no intention of committing to anyone ever. A playboy, as Sydney accused when we met.

My life was crafted to be fun, stimulating, and unpredictable on purpose. It's what the four of us guys wanted. To constantly be on the go and have endless adventures together. But lately, all that excitement has lost its luster, its appeal. The second I saw Sydney carrying that ridiculous armload of books, I was struck. Like Cupid's cheesy arrow in cartoons or Valentine's Day cards.

But I can't think about her right now. She affects my system too much, and I need to focus on getting through this torture race. Then, I see her. Her bright red hair flows in the breeze as she bounces. She's smiling and holding a sign above her head, but I can't tear my eyes from her face long enough to read it.

She's yelling something I can't process through the crowd noise or the fog her presence creates. As I jog closer, I slow down, but the runner behind me doesn't get the message. He slams into me, and I stagger forward, catching myself on the asphalt with a palm before my knees hit. Ignoring the pain, I jump up and search through the sea of faces.

She's gone.

"Shit." I double over, resting my aching palms on my aching knees. Who have I become? The woman has my balls cupped in her hands, and I can barely function.

"Mason!" I hear someone call from up the street.

I shake my head, not daring to look. There's only one person who calls me that, but I can't face the disappointment of seeing her again only to have her disappear.

"I have fudge," she yells over the noise, bringing a relieved smile to my face.

"What kind?" I respond without moving.

"Chocolate with marshmallows and walnuts."

"That's my favorite."

"I know."

Taking in a deep breath, I rise, and my eyes land on her instantly. She's holding a small plastic container and the sign I saw her with moments ago. So, I'm not crazy after all.

I read the words printed in big bold letters on the sign:

I LOVE MY MARINE
MORE THAN FUDGE

With a laugh, I jog to her. My hands go to her face and kiss the lips I've missed to the infinite power. "More than fudge, huh?" I whisper, resting my forehead against hers. "That's a lot because I know how much you love fudge."

She nods, seemingly as breathless from our kiss as I am.

"I can't believe you're here." I lean back to see the eyes that have kept me going each day since leaving Richmond. Other than memory, all I have is a picture of her on my phone. It's not the same. "I thought you had plans."

"This was that plan. I wanted to surprise you. Nora and Denise are here, too."

"Oh," I say, dropping my hands to her arms.

"Don't worry. They know I'm here only to be with you."

"Good." I smile and look around. "Come with me."

"Where?"

Taking her hand, I push through the crowd until finding a secluded area behind a row of evergreen trees. When we're hidden away, she drops the sign and container of fudge to leap into my arms. Our lips come together as her arms and legs wrap around me. The moment we touch, I'm weak from wanting her and not being able to have her all these weeks.

Stepping forward, I gently press her back to a large tree trunk and soak in all she's willing to give. And she's generous. For what seems like hours, we kiss and touch and relish this moment. It's one that will be etched into my memory forever.

"Sydney," I manage, using all the willpower I can muster to separate from her.

"Yes?" she responds with an airy sigh, and I wait for her eyelids slowly flutter open.

"I am so hopelessly in love with you."

"I know," she says with a grin and takes my mouth again with more force and passion than I knew was possible.

I'm fully prepared to stay here in this tree line for however long she's willing to be with me like this. And all I can think through the haze she creates—other than calculating the quickest route to my hotel room—is she better be in this for the long haul because I'm never letting her go.

―――

Jackson: Are you dead? You should have been here an hour ago. You're slow, but not this slow.

Will: Ha. Ha.

Jackson: Hurry up. I've got a three-beer head start. If you don't get here soon, you'll never catch up. Kind of like when we run.

Will: You're hilarious. Had a few distractions.

Jackson: Not again. I'm rolling my eyes right now, but you probably already knew that. She coming with you?

Will: Be there soon.

Chapter Sixteen

✯ ✯ ✯

Will

By the time I arrive, Jackson's sitting at the largest table in the room and Marines occupy every seat but one. Some we know from past deployments and some from the academy. Others we've met along the way at events like the half-marathon or during training. By the look of things already, it's sure to be a long and rowdy night.

Usually, that would excite me, motivate me. It's a luxury not afforded to every Marine to attend these events—I'm lucky to have a high-ranking best friend—but despite that, I can't wait for it to be over.

Sydney and her friends are sitting across the bar at their own table. She knows I haven't told Jackson about her yet and suggested we stay incognito until I'm ready. I don't know why I'm still struggling to say the words to him. If I did, I could address it and get it over with.

It can't be fear. I'm afraid of nothing. Well, now that I think about it, that's changed, too. I'm terrified of losing Sydney. Scared of not coming back from this next deployment and how that would hurt her.

I can't be holding back simply because Jackson's never seen me have feelings for someone. Hell, I never wanted to, and we joke about it often, but this change in me isn't that big of a deal. Not enough to keep the words from being spoken. Jackson and I tell each other everything. He understands me and supports me no matter what, as I do him. So, why can't I tell him about falling in love for the first time? About this life-changing experience?

Maybe that's it. Maybe I'm afraid of something else. Of losing my three friends. To be with Sydney, I'd have to leave the service and my friends. The guys and I have done everything together since we were kids. Same classes, same sports. Trips, family, hobbies, life, career. All of it.

When I choose Sydney, will they understand? And when I go, who am I without them? Without the service? Will I still be the same person Sydney fell in love with? Whatever it is, I can't keep standing here like a fool. There are months between now and deployment. I'll figure it out.

Coming up behind Jackson, I slap him on the back to announce my presence.

"It's about time you got here. I was beginning to worry," he says and hands me a beer from the iced bucket sitting on the table.

"I took my time since I knew I couldn't beat you."

"No one can," Marvin, a recent retiree, announces. "Many have tried. All have failed. How are you, Will?" He rises from his seat and reaches out a hand.

"I'm great. How's the civilian life?"

"After thirty years in the Corps, it's pretty damn sweet," he begins and returns to his seat as I take the last empty chair. "The wife and I are watching the grandkids a lot and traveling in our new RV. We sleep in and eat whatever we want. I highly recommend it."

That moment—it's the first time any part of the civilian lifestyle sounded appealing. What Marvin described sounds like heaven with Sydney. I want to do all those things with her. Eventually, I'll tell the guys, then ask her to marry me. I'll retire like Marvin and live every day to put a smile on her beautiful face.

Eight years of service is a respectable amount to give your country. Jackson won't be happy at first, but he'll come around and support my decision. He won't have a choice since he'll be the best man in our wedding. Plus, he'll still have Billy and Josh to travel and run with at the ass-crack of dawn.

My face must have given me away because Jackson asks, "What are you grinning about?"

"A woman, probably," Benji chimes in. He served under Jackson during our last tour and knows us well.

"You're just jealous," I jokingly accuse.

"Damn right, I am. If I looked like you and Jackson, I'd be under a gorgeous woman every chance I got, too."

"For the record, I don't operate like that, and Jackson's practically celibate."

Benji makes a tsking sound and shakes his head. "Such a waste, but I know from experience that's not the whole truth."

As the group erupts into laughter in unison, then settles back into their conversations, my eyes find Sydney across the bar. It's easy to tune out my surroundings with her in my sights. She must have felt me watching since she turns and meets my gaze.

My leg starts bouncing to the music, and I can't seem to stop fidgeting with my beer bottle. It's full since my body is begging for her and not the alcohol. I shoot up out of my seat, no longer concerned about who sees me with her.

"I'll be back."

"Where are you off to already?" Marvin asks.

Then, as I stalk away, my eyes zeroed in on the target, I hear someone answer, "You know where. There must be a super-model who needs his attention. Bring back a few for us," they yell after me.

It takes me no time at all to reach her table.

"Well, hello there, handsome," she greets, keeping her body language casual.

"Hi," I say to Sydney, then the others so as not to ignore them. My mother raised a gentleman, after all.

"You remember Denise, don't you?"

"Of course." I turn to Denise. "Thank you for your help."

"Help?" Sydney asks. "What did you—? Oh. You were the one to spill the beans about my work schedule."

Guilt rises into her cheeks. "I would say I'm sorry, but I'm not."

"I would say I'm mad at you…but I'm not." Sydney laughs, then returns her attention to me. "Are you here to join us?"

"Or," Denise chimes in, "are you here to introduce us to all those manly Marines I see at your table?"

"I *was* ordered to bring back some beautiful ladies with me, and I never disobey orders." I look down at Sydney. She's grinning, no doubt thinking what I'm thinking. With her friends occupied, we can disappear. No one will think anything of it. *Classic Will*, they'll say, shaking their heads. "I'll hang out here for a moment if you don't mind. Put on a little show for the guys. Then, I'll take you over."

"So, which ones are single? Start with the hottest ones first," Denise instructs. There's not a subtle bone in her body.

"I'm not exactly well-versed in judging male hotness. Which ones would you like to meet?" I ask and sit down beside Sydney, placing my hand on her thigh beneath the table. With her hand resting on mine, I relax while Denise studies my friends and acquaintances across the room.

"Well," she begins. "Any man in a military uniform gets the downstairs juices flowing." She raises her eyebrows a few times at us before continuing her evaluation. "Let's start with the one on the far left. On the end. He looks like a twenty out of ten."

I check the table again. "Jackson? Yeah, most women say that."

"Do I detect a bit of jealousy?"

"Not in the least. I've been known to hold my own beside him."

Denise shrugs without taking her eyes off the other table. "I would have given you an eighteen. Close enough, but no cigar." She cuts her eyes to me and smiles.

"That's fair, but don't waste your time. He's married to the Marines and is as faithful as a monk."

"Boring. What about the sexy, dark-headed one next to him?"

I check again. "That's Benji. Life of the party, affectionate, good dancer. You'll like him."

"Who's the blond, second from the right, facing us?" Nora asks, biting her bottom lip.

After a glance and a count from the right, I answer. "That's Lawrence. I don't know much about him other than he's a decorated sniper."

"That's impressive, but I imagine there's a lot of baggage that comes along with that."

"You imagine correctly."

"Sad. Who do you think I'd like and vice versa?" Nora asks.

"Are you looking for a weekend meet-up or something more long-term?"

"Hey," Denise protests. "Why didn't you ask me that question?"

"Because he already has you pegged," Sydney says, then throws her head back laughing. Nora soon joins in.

"It's not my fault there are too many gorgeous men in uniform. I need to try them all to see which one fits…you know, long term." She scowls, then pinches back a guilty smile. "Monogamy is overrated."

"What did you tell me, Nora?" Sydney urges.

"We're only twenty-two…blah blah blah. A stress-free weekend romance sounds amazing." She slumps back in her seat, snatching her drink off the table with the motion.

"Alright. I think you'd hit it off with Jones. He's your age and—"

"Jones?"

"Jordan Jones," I clarify. "Everyone calls him by his last name because there was already a Jordan on the squad, and he has seniority."

"Perfect," Denise chimes in and leans her elbow on the table. "Have we wasted enough time yet?"

Chapter Seventeen

✫ ✫ ✫

Sydney

While Will plays matchmaker, I wait for him at the table, anxiously sipping my fruity pink drink. I have no idea what it's called. Nora bought it at the bar while I saved a table for us. It has rum, raspberry and orange juices with a fresh pineapple slice sitting on the edge of the glass.

By the time I drain the last drop of fruity deliciousness and start playing with the little yellow umbrella, Will returns and rushes me out of the bar. And rush isn't an exaggeration. Our pace is just short of a brisk jog.

"Aren't you tired?" I ask an hour later. We had been lying on the bed since we arrived at the hotel, tucked comfortably in each other's arms and talking.

"No. Being with you always gives me energy."

He kisses my forehead, and the tenderness he shows me makes me swoon. "Good. When can I come see you at the base?"

"Anytime you want. I just need to check the schedule."

"What about Jackson and the guys?"

"Don't care anymore. I'll tell them eventually, but they probably won't believe me."

I sit up. "Why not? Wait, don't answer that." I go to lie back down, but he stops me by placing a finger under my chin. His eyes are laser-focused on mine and deadly serious.

"Sydney. I love you. Nothing I've done in the past matters. It's not who I am anymore."

"I know." I flash a grin to accompany my usual response. "Oh! I have something for you."

"You do?"

I push to my knees and reach into the back pocket of my shorts while he readjusts to lean back against the headboard. Then, I hold up my thumb, showcasing the black band around the base.

"What's that?"

"It's a promise ring. Nothing fancy, but since it's made of rubber, I thought you might be able to wear it sometimes." I wiggle the band off my thumb and place it on my palm. "It also has a message engraved on the inside."

Taking the ring, he examines the tiny message. "Is it Gaelic?"

"Yes. *Mo grá thú*."

"What's it mean?"

"I love you. This ring is a symbol of my promise to love you forever."

At that, his eyes raise to mine, but he doesn't move.

"You're not the only one who gets to make promises in this relationship," I say to fill the silence. I can't tell if he's rendered speechless or trying to determine if I mean it.

The sides of his mouth slowly pull into a wide smile before he lunges at me and takes possession of my lips. The force pushes me onto my back, like that fateful day on the grass outside my apartment. Except this time, I'm not fighting it. My heart is his. And here, in the privacy of his hotel room, I'm ready for him to have the rest of me.

I place a palm on his chest to put some space between us. His heart is racing, and his eyes are hazy, but I need him to hear me. "I want to tell you something."

"Not yet."

"What?"

He rolls onto his side and holds up the ring with his thumb and forefinger. "I don't want to lose this." He slides it on his right ring finger, then pounces on me again.

A squeal escapes, but his lips connecting with mine once more eclipse the sound.

"Will, wait." I exhale and pull back, already regretting the decision, but I need to get this out in the open.

"But I was just getting started."

That makes me smile. "Good, because I want to be with you tonight." I press a finger to his lips when he opens his mouth to me again: *Are you sure? Will you regret this tomorrow?* "Yes, I'm sure, and I definitely will never regret it. Who knows when we might see each other again. I can't wait until then. Show me how much you love me, Will. I want to feel it. Feel you."

———

"The world did not prepare me for you," Will says, breathless and sweating. He kisses my forehead and pulls me closer inside the hot sheets.

"The Irish are good at more than just drinking and eating."

"I don't know about the rest of the population, but you, my sweet, must be the champion."

I giggle, happier than I ever knew was possible. "You're biased."

"Maybe, but now we know we work together out there and in here."

"Yes, we do." I pop up, kiss his cheek, and return to snuggling beside him.

"See? We're meant to be. Worth the risk. Dangerous or not."

"You're even more dangerous now. How am I supposed to focus on anything else?" With a laugh, I throw back the sheet and climb on top of him.

"Pretty soon, you won't have to."

"What?"

He tucks the hair cascading around his face behind my ear before running a finger lightly down my neck.

"After this tour, I'm leaving the Marines."

His finger trails across my collarbone and between my breasts, his eyes following.

"What do you mean?" Secretly, I'm praying it means what I think it does.

His eyes shoot to mine. "It means I'm choosing you. I want to spend every minute I can by your side for the rest of my life."

"What?" I didn't intend to ask it again, but I need to make sure I heard him right.

"I'm retiring as soon as I'm able." His hand raises to my cheek. "Thanks to you, I want to get married, have a family and a little house in the country. I never wanted that before."

"Will, I—"

"Is that not what you want?"

I'll never forget the way his eyes changed when he asked that. How they clouded with pain at the thought of losing me. Whatever I have to do, I'll do it to make sure he never feels that way again.

"Will, no. I mean, of course I want all of that with you. But is leaving what *you* want? I'll never forgive myself if you leave before you're ready just to make me happy."

He sits up and wraps his arms around me. For a long while, he holds me—his cheek pressed against my chest. I wonder what he's thinking. Is he weighing his options? Thinking about his dreams, friends, and the adventures he'd miss out on?

"This is what I want," he whispers finally. "Nothing else matters."

"You're very cute when you sleep," Will says when I open my eyes and find him watching me.

"Ugh." I roll into his chest.

"No. Don't you ever hide." Gently, he pushes on my shoulder to expose my groggy, make-up-free face. "You're too beautiful. Too special. Never believe anything else."

Reaching up to cup my hand behind his neck, I pull him down to me. "I love you."

"I love you and my promise ring. I'll never take it off unless Sgt. Jackson is rude and makes me."

I let out a giggle. "When do you leave?"

"He's expecting me to meet him in the lobby in thirty minutes."

"Thirty minutes? Why didn't you wake me up?"

"I told you. You were too cute, and I figured after last night, you needed to rest."

I smack his chest, but he catches my wrist and pulls me on top of him.

"Well, this doesn't seem fair. You're already dressed."

"And you're stunning in this light." His eyes travel down my body and back to meet my gaze. "I want to commit every inch of you to memory to help get me through these next few months."

"Well, hopefully soon, you won't have to remember. You can look and touch all you want."

He stares at me a moment. "Have I told you lately how much I love you?"

"Yes," I giggle again before turning on my most sultry voice. I'm not ready to let him go yet. "Only about twenty times, and you were masterful when you *showed* me three times. I, my love, am a very lucky and satisfied girl." I lean down to plant a kiss on his soft lips, hoping to ignite another spark.

"There's time for me to show you one more time, if you're interested."

And just like that, the spark flares into a blazing fire. "I will never turn that down. Show me, Mason. I want to feel your love."

———

My Sweet Sydney,

   I'm so sorry that I haven't been able to find any free time for your visit over these past few months. Believe me, I have tried everything. I even thought about playing sick, but Jackson would never buy it. I'd have to be on my deathbed before he'd let me skip training.

   I miss you so much it hurts. The guys have noticed a change in me, but they haven't pressed me on it. There's too much to do to get ready for deployment that we don't have time to dwell on anything non-mission related. Speaking of that, Jackson informed us today that we fly out November 2nd.

   One month. One month to find an escape back to your arms and one last moment of peace. I'm having a hard time sleeping without you beside me. Food and beer have lost their appeal, and all I want is to hold you again. But I don't know if I'll get another chance to do that before we leave. For that, I'm sorry. I'm sorry I couldn't keep my promise to you.

   But I hope you know how hard I tried. How much I am still trying. Getting to you is all I think about. All I want is to be with you.

   I love you.
   Will

Chapter Eighteen

✯ ✯ ✯

Sydney

I've always hated autumn—the dying season. It's the time of dull earth tones, musty smells, and inescapable blah. Leaves take their last breath through vibrant colors before plummeting to the ground, only to be stepped on and discarded like everyone hadn't just marveled at them for weeks before that.

Sad jack-o-lantern faces rolling in on themselves and decaying in the cool, damp air. Even the daylight seems dimmer, muted. But even more than that, I despise how the warm colors of my Irish skin and red hair blend in with my surroundings. The last thing I want is to blend in with anything (Will's demand), but this stupid time of year gives me no choice.

Today feels no different. But at least, as I walk across the Richmond University campus, the air smells a little sweeter. A breeze tickles my face, like cotton candy does when you bite the fluffy sugar off the stiff paper handle. Maybe it's the five-pound bag of chocolate I'm carrying or the melted caramel at the candy apple stand warming in the pot and waiting for the next order.

Every stand I pass on the way to the commons area between the cafeteria and library offers a different cavity-inducing creation. Funnel cakes, kettle corn, baked goods, homemade candy, or flavored drinks. The annual RU Halloween Festival is buzzing with activity, but I can't wait to go home.

I've lost interest in doing anything outside the necessary. School, work, waiting for an update from Will, lying awake all night. Repeat. Every minute of every day, I wish he was here.

He has a way of making me forget that I am fall's camouflage. His kiss helps me smell roses and sugar instead of mold and decay. Probably because he always brings flowers and fudge, but even if he didn't, the days and nights are better when he's in them.

"Oh, thank goodness," Nora says, snatching the bag from my tired arms and ripping it open.

I walked from the general store a block outside of campus, about a mile from the festival, and my arms feel like cooked spaghetti again. Never did get to those push-ups in the midst of all the sulking.

"What's a Halloween display without candy?" she asks.

"Boring."

"Exactly."

I watch her dump half the bag into the large orange bowl surrounded by plastic spiders, then toss it under the table.

"What's your goal here?" I ask, studying the signs and decorations.

"To get students to complete our survey about campus life."

Nora works part-time in the Office of Student Relations when she isn't waitressing.

"Well, in that costume, the entire male student population will be stopping by tonight. Your survey results may be skewed." I raise my brow at her sexy witch costume, complete with a black mini skirt—ripped and jagged on the ends—fishnet hose, knee-high boots, and a black skin-tight T-shirt that plunges low enough to reveal at least four inches of her bountiful cleavage. Her dark makeup only highlights her plump lips and big blue eyes. The charcoal shadow and mascara make the light color of her irises almost look translucent in contrast. She's stunning. "They'll be doing more drooling on the survey than actually filling it out."

With a mischievous grin, she places a hand under each breast and pushes up. "I can be very persuasive."

"Oh, no doubt. Speaking of persuasion, have you responded to any of Jordan's texts and calls? Will mentioned that Jordan's still hoping to keep in touch."

"I bet he is," she mumbles.

Knowing what happened that weekend between them in Fredericksburg, I decide to ignore the comment. Nora used to give me a hard time about my dating ban, but she's just as reluctant to start a relationship as I was. She may not call it the same or name it at all, but it's a ban no matter how she describes it.

I walk around the table, fanning myself along the way, and drop my purse on the remnant candy bag. Although the air was cool, the trek from the store to this table was long, and I was sweating by the time I arrived.

"Why won't you give him a chance?" I ask. She's intrigued by him as he is with her, but she won't admit it and loosen her fool-proof grip on her heart.

"What?" Nora stares at me like I asked her to do something ridiculous and unfathomable.

"For one, I'm not going to answer that. I said I wanted a weekend fling, not a boyfriend. Second, do not tell me you dressed as an Irish maiden tonight."

I look down at my green and black plaid pleated skirt and knee-high green socks and smirk. "Okay. I won't."

She scowls, not appreciating my joke or my butting in about Jordan. "I thought you were more creative than that," she accuses.

"Under normal circumstances, I would be. But—"

"No time for making a costume when you're moping, huh?"

"Not exactly," I protest, crossing my arms to look more convincing. "I've had to work and study and…"

"Mope," Nora says again, not buying my act.

Surrendering, I drop my arms and lean on the table. "Something like that." Even the romance novels, journaling, and Nora's therapy sessions aren't helping.

"This is exactly why I won't get involved with Jordan. I liked him. He got the juices flowing, but if I let myself go there, I'll end up like you."

"Thanks a lot." I snatch a tiny candy bar from the bowl, yank off the wrapper and toss it in my mouth.

"Um, Sydney?"

"Yeah?" I respond with gooey caramel and nougat stuck in my teeth.

"Didn't you say Will took care of the Trevor problem?"

"Yeah." The question catches me off guard. Nora sat on the bathroom floor with me while I cried ugly tears night after night following my breakup with Trevor. She knows Will punched him after our dinner date and the demands he made of Trevor. "Why?"

She continues to contemplate, her gaze on something over my shoulder. "He's headed this way, and his eyes are locked on a certain short plaid skirt."

I don't dare look. "You're lying."

"Would I lie to you?"

"He must be eyeing the candy or your mile of cleavage."

She scowls at me. "Nope. You remember that documentary we watched the other day?"

"The one about the Sahara Desert?" I ask, confused about the strange, random question.

"Yeah. He's the lion and you're the gazelle. He's on a mission to devour you."

"What the hell? Don't tell him Will is gone," I demand quickly. "I need him to—owwah. What was that for?" I rub my arm where Nora's bony elbow poked me.

"Hi, Sydney."

I close my eyes at the sound of the familiar voice behind me. What is he doing here? Doesn't he remember his busted nose and the reason for it?

"What do you want, Trevor?" Nora chimes in, trying to protect the pitiful person I used to be with him. But the task of reconstructing myself and being with Will has shown me who I truly am. I'm stronger than I realize.

"Nora, I've got this." I spin around and put on my most indifferent expression, which is quite tricky considering his ridiculous costume. He is wearing a white toga, sandals, and a homemade laurel wreath on his head…so frat boy cliché. And standing behind him are two matching toga boys. A triplet cliché. "Trevor."

"You're looking beautiful tonight," he says with an arrogant grin. Like this is a game and he's skirting the rules.

"Are we really doing this again?" I hope my tone spells it out for him. I'm so over his emotional tear me down, build me back up rollercoaster ride. When we were together, he mastered the art of knocking my legs out from under me and holding me down where I crash-landed. But he doesn't realize that since then, I've uncovered the truth about how I deserve to be treated. How it feels to be treasured, appreciated, and protected by a real man.

Never again will Trevor affect me, hold anything over me, hurt me, or change me.

"Can't I give a friend a compliment when I see her?" he asks, undeterred.

"We're not friends, Trevor. Not after the way you set that bridge on fire on your way out the door and especially after what you did last spring."

He studies me, letting his eyes rake over my body, and a chill runs down my back from how dirty that makes me feel.

When his gaze returns to mine, I'm stone-faced. He's yet to apologize for how he ended things or show the least bit of remorse for hurting me.

His chin lifts in defiance. "What are you talking about?"

"You know exactly what I'm talking about. Just leave me alone or your face may not fare so well next time."

Amused by his gaping mouth reaction, my lips pinch into a flat grin before turning to Nora. "If you'll excuse me, I have somewhere to be."

I snatch up my purse, not waiting for a response, and stroll away. At least, I hope it looks like I'm strolling. My heart is pounding so hard it's making me dizzy. I probably look drunk from their perspective, but I don't care.

Seeing him again is not top of my list of fun things to do on a Friday night. Or any night for that matter. Damn him for ruining my flailing efforts to maintain a positive mood. Now I miss Will even more, and I'm angry that he's not here and Trevor is. It's not fair.

My feet are carrying me faster than my energy level can support. When I'm out of sight of Nora's table, I stop and rest a hand against a brick building. I'm stronger than this. Terrible Trevor, as Nora once called him, isn't worth a freakout. I'm over him. He means nothing.

Picking up my heavy heart, I trudge on. I'll feel better once I'm in some comfy flannel pajamas and getting lost in a good book. When I set out that night for the festival, I thought spending time with Nora around the holiday festivities would smack me out of my brooding.

Thank you, Trevor, for ruining that, too.

After exiting campus, I stop outside the fudge shop that happens to be on my broody path to the apartment. Maybe my longing for Will sent me here. Thinking of him and the many times he brought me fudge from this very shop has tears flooding my eyes.

He's probably unavailable, but I snap a photo of me outside the shop, red face and all, and send it to him with a short message.

Sydney: Thinking of you.

I didn't expect to receive a message back and especially not immediately. Seeing his name pop up on the phone, I sit on a dainty metal chair outside the shop ready for my frustrations to be soothed by his sweet words.

Will: All the gooey marshmallowy chocolate fudge in the world could never be as sweet as you.

Will: What are you up to?

Sydney: Halloween Festival was a disaster. Heading home. Saw fudge. Legs stopped working.

Will: You look like you've been crying. Everything okay?

Sydney: Saw fudge. Thought of you. Cried.

Will: I'm sorry for ruining it for you. Why was the festival a disaster?

Sydney: Ran into Trevor.

Will: Trevor's there? Are you alone?

Will: Sydney!

Sydney: Yes. I'm fine. He was on his way to a party with some frat boys.

Will: Cowards grow balls when they have backup. Please go straight home. Watch your back. Don't open the door for anyone.

Sydney: I know you're trying to protect me, but I'll be okay. Please don't worry.

Will: Can't help it. If anything happens to you…

Sydney: I love you.

Will: Love you, too.

Sydney: Getting many pounds of fudge now.

A lot of chocolatey deliciousness sounds like the perfect complement to flannels and steamy romance novels. I'm sure I'll regret the calories tomorrow, but as I step inside, the sweet smell of sugar and warm sweetness fills my soul and lightens my sour mood instantly. Most any problem can be fixed with chocolate. Am I right?

"Sydney?"

Seriously?! That judgmental tone is like mistaking salt for sugar when making sweet tea. I've done it, and my body is reacting to my mother's voice in the same way it did when I took that first repulsive sip of tea-flavored salt water.

Since she would not appreciate being ignored, which was my first thought, I reluctantly turn from the case of sugary heaven that promised to make me feel better. But it's a good thing I haven't made the purchase yet. After this conversation, I'll need at least two pounds of fudge to accomplish that. Maybe three.

"Hi, Mom," I say with a quick exhale and my best fake smile. "What are you doing down here?"

"Well, I needed some chocolate for a cake I'm making for the church bake sale on Sunday, and a new spoon. Your father broke the good one we brought from Dublin." Her eyes roll to show her disgust.

My father is a brute of a man. Strong as an ox, hence the broken spoon, except where his overbearing, never satisfied wife is concerned. He's loyal and never wavers from her side. Which was quite frustrating growing up, especially when he refused to take my side when I was right.

"I'm sorry to hear that," I try to empathize to keep our conversation from going down the usual exasperating path.

"You know him. Always taking my good bowls and utensils to use in his garden. Now, I have to settle for an American spoon." American anything pales in comparison to Irish-made in her opinion. "When will you be coming home for a visit? It's been months since you stopped by."

My fingers shoot to my lips, and I chew a nail. It's a nervous reflex anytime *home* is mentioned. Wouldn't it be nice if home was a comfort like it was at Will's house? A place I could go to soothe my aching heart. But instead, it only adds more of that pesky salt because I'll never live up to my mother's expectations.

"I'm not sure. I've got class and work—"

"Work," she scoffs.

By now you'd think I would know when to keep my mouth shut. I'm so annoying.

"At your age, I was married and pregnant with your brother," she continues, undeterred by my lack of interest. I've heard this diatribe a hundred times. It only reinforces my desire to do the exact opposite of whatever she says. "That's the role our good Lord wants for us. You should be making things right with Trevor. He would provide a great home for a family."

I puff out my displeasure at that vastly misinformed statement. "Trevor is the last person I want to be tied to for the rest of my life. I don't love him."

"What does love have to do with having a good marriage?"

I don't react to that last question because she's quick to bring it up whenever she hears I'm dating. *What does he offer? Can he pay the bills? Would he be a disciplinarian for your children? Does he follow the good teachings of the Bible?* That's all she's ever concerned with. You'd think we lived in the far distant past.

"Mother, it's late and I'm tired. Can we talk about this later?"

"Fine. But Trevor would make a fine husband, and you wouldn't have to work or waste your time going to school."

"College is not a waste of time. Not that you would understand." That slipped out despite knowing better, but she was exhausting my patience and my tongue gets loose when I run out.

"Don't tell me what I don't understand." She waves her long bony finger in my direction. A warning I know all too well. "I've seen and lived more than you, young lady, and you'd be smart to heed my advice."

"You're right. I'm sorry," I cave in hopes of ending this embarrassing scene. "I should get back to helping Nora at the festival." It's a lie but saying that I want to go to the apartment she forbade me from getting will only start another lecture. I'm sinful, I get it. Now, leave me be. "Tell Da I said hi, and I'll stop by soon."

I wrap my arms around her frigid shoulders, but she doesn't reach out. Only stands there like a cold, metal pole. But I've come to expect that reaction, too. Am I really that much of a disappointment?

I forgo the mood-improving fudge and escape the shop before she finds a way to answer that metaphorical question. Plus, the fudge would only be useless calories at this point. Nothing can lift my spirits now. Except Will, but he's not here.

More salt for my wounded heart.

Chapter Nineteen

✯ ✯ ✯

Sydney

The walk home took longer than usual because my legs ached as much as my heart. I also had to stop to answer two texts from Nora and three more from Will. He's still worried about Trevor following me home. But I'm convinced the nose punch knocked that idea right out of his arrogant head.

"Hi, Mr. Darcy," I say when the little dog shoots by my feet at the base of the apartment stairs. "Stupid dog. You're no smarter than I am. You never will learn."

Ignoring him, I continue up the first flight of stairs and run into Ms. Stanley at the turn between the first and second floors.

"Hello, Ms.—"

"Hi, Sweetie. Can't talk right now," she huffs on her way by.

"Good evening to you, too," I joke to myself, now wishing I had bought that fudge. Maybe I'll try to make my own. I bought all the ingredients shortly after our cooking lesson with Caroline, but I haven't had the nerve to make it. It just wouldn't be the same without her or Will. And I'd probably ruin it, anyway. Like the sweet tea debacle.

Stepping onto the balcony leading to my apartment, I freeze when my eyes land on a tall figure leaning against the rail outside my door. Only a few outside lights are on, mostly because they don't work, and I can't see his face in the shadows.

The figure straightens when he sees me, and defensively, I step back. Had Trevor come here, knowing I'd be alone? Vulnerable?

"Stop right there," I demand, gripping my bag and wondering if there's anything in there to protect me.

"Sydney, it's me."

"Will?"

He steps into the one light on the balcony that works, confirming my daily wish has come true. Tears pool in my eyes at the sight of him. My heart expands, and I can't inhale. Can't move my heavy legs. I'm desperate to run to him. To be enveloped in the love and safety of his arms. But all I can do is collapse, my hands covering my face as the dam breaks.

Rushing closer, he kneels in front of me. "Baby, what's the matter?"

"I wished for you tonight, never expecting you to actually come." I look up and tears stream down my cold cheeks. "How are you here?"

"They decided to give us a couple days off before we go." He sweeps the hair from my forehead and plants a kiss there.

"Why didn't you tell me earlier?"

"I was hoping to surprise you, and I was at the mercy of Josh's snail driving."

A laugh-snort escapes my throat, but I don't care. "Does he know?"

"Yes."

"Good job."

"I had to tell him to get here faster, but he's sworn to secrecy." His hands move to my elbows, and we stand together. "Come here."

He pulls me into his arms, and I melt into him, his scent, his love. "God, I've missed this," I whisper against his chest.

He kisses my head again and runs a hand down my back. "You look really hot in this outfit."

A half chuckle slips out. "Thanks. Nora said it was disappointing."

"Not possible. Is she still at the festival?"

I lean back to see his face. His eyes are filled with desire. "Yes. How are you going to take advantage of this alone time?"

"Well, I will fix you a glass of wine, massage your sore feet, run a hot bubble bath, and kiss every inch of you until you feel better."

"Will you be in that bubble bath with me?"

"If you want. Or I will sit beside the tub and rub your shoulders or wash your hair. Tonight is all about you and what you want."

"What if I want to make love until dawn and all day tomorrow." I smile up at him, and he lowers to press his lips to mine. He lingers until I start to squirm.

"Then, I'll have to suck it up for your happiness," he answers before releasing me. "You're in charge."

"That's what I want. But *after* that glass of wine, foot massage and bubble bath you promised. I want all of you for as long as we have together."

―――

"How is this possible?" Will asks, his fingers pressed to his lips as he looks me over.

I pause, letting my helmet straps swing in the breeze with my hair. "What?"

"You're making that dull, scratched-up helmet look sexy."

"Such the charmer," I dismiss, continuing to fidget with the rough straps of the full-body apparatus I'm wearing. It must weigh more than I do, and the material is irritating my shoulders.

But leave it to Will to turn an ordinary task into a lesson in sex appeal. His eyes lock on mine as he takes hold of the buckle under my chin. It clicks into place, and his knuckles brush against my jawline, lingering there long enough to send an electric pulse through my entire body. Then, my sanity falters when he hooks a finger around the clip at the center of my harness. With one gentle tug, I fall forward into his arms and that's all it takes for me to go mad with desire.

He tilts his head, and I await the kiss his eyes are promising. The kiss I need more than air to breathe. But instead, he says, "Ready for this?"

A sudden gush of fear lodges in my throat, suffocating my excitement for other things. "Whose idea was it to go bungee jumping?"

"Yours."

I drop my forehead to his chest. "Oh, right."

"We can back out," he suggests. "Try something a little more low-key like putt-putt golf or go-carts." He pinches back a smile at what he knows I will take as a challenge.

"Shut up."

With that settled, he doesn't hesitate. "We're ready," he informs the attendee, who is joining the last clips on our individual harnesses.

This is a couple's jump, advertised as romantic and memorable in the Adventure Park brochure. But I'm catching none of those feels now that it's go-time. My heart is pumping at an unhealthy rate, and I'm sweating despite the cool fall breeze at this ridiculous altitude.

"Gotcha, Boss," the attendant responds, kicking the elastic cord aside. "You're good to go."

"What? Just like that?" I complain, forgetting to keep my I've-got-this composure.

Ignoring my flailing confidence, Will lifts me up with one arm and shuffles to the designated spot at the opening. As he sets me down, I look at the splotchy green and blah grass far below and wonder what's come over me.

This morning, I suggested coming to the Adventure Park to give us something fun and exciting to do on our last day together. Something we'll always remember. Now, thinking about the three hundred-plus-foot free fall we're about to take, I wish we'd stayed in the safe, warm bed. We could be snuggling under the blankets right now with the fresh batch of fudge we made last night.

Now, *that* is a moment I will never forget. When the late-night munchies hit, we decided to test what we learned and make some fudge. It took longer than necessary since we couldn't keep our hands off each other, and we had to keep quiet so we didn't wake Nora. We felt like disobedient teenagers, sneaking about the house, tiptoeing and giggling at the absurdity of it all. But I will forever be in love with making love while making fudge.

Who does that? Well, Will and I do, and I'll never look at marshmallow cream the same way ever again.

"Sydney," Will says, breaking the tension building in my chest. I meet his gaze, and time seems to hesitate. "I've got you, but you're just as brave and infallible as most of the Marines I know. You can do anything. I'm here, but you don't need me."

"I will always need you," I admit softly on an exhale.

At that, he smiles and takes my face in his hands. "Ready?"

I nod and repeat, "I can do anything. I am a survivor."

"Damn, right you are."

With Will by my side, I believe every word. Rising to my toes, I press a kiss to his lips, wrap my arms around his waist and pull him overboard. A scream is muffled in my throat as I press harder against him. What is it with us? We're always flying, floating, or falling. But isn't that the perfect representation of our love story? Free and unrestrained.

We drift for only seconds before we're yanked back up again and that's when he deepens the kiss. The second recoil barely registers, and I'm engulfed in the thrill of being connected to Will in this way. Of creating this unforgettable memory together.

Looks like the brochure was right. The couple's bungee jump takes the romance to an entirely new level. Literally.

As we're lowered to the landing pad, our lips still connected, it takes a minute to realize we're not alone. The crew and spectators surrounding the platform begin clapping and whistling and whooping as if we had put on a show.

Well, maybe we set off some fireworks on the way down. I certainly felt a few rockets soaring along the way.

Will jumps up and pulls me to my feet, but while the crew unbuckles our harnesses, his fingers stay laced with mine. I can feel his reluctance to let go and can empathize. Neither of us wants this moment or this day to end.

"How about some hot chocolate?" he asks when we're released.

"That sounds amazing."

―――

"Zipline, ropes course, go-carts, arcade, or bungee jumping. Which was your favorite?" Will asks after we claim a table by the fireplace in the lodge overlooking the ski slopes. It's only grassy hills at this time of year, but soon, it will be buzzing with enthusiastic skiers.

While I take a moment to consider his question, I gaze out the window at the beautiful fall day. Most of the leaves on the surrounding trees are bare, except for the evergreens lining the areas cleared for skiing. The tall bungee platform is peeking over the edge of snow tubing lanes in the distance on the left and the putt-putt course behind it. I love it here and can see myself coming back to feel closer to Will while he's away.

"Well," I finally say, turning around to face him and leaning on the windowsill. "It's a toss-up between beating you at skeeball and making out with you on the bungee."

"Let me get this straight. Rolling a ball into a circle is as much fun to you as being lip locked with the handsomest guy you know while swinging in the air three hundred feet off the ground?"

"What can I say? I'm very competitive, and you're cute when you pout." I wink over my mug before taking a sip of the hot, creamy liquid.

He straightens in protest. "I never pout."

"Then what was all that complaining you did about your ball being lopsided or your lane uneven?" His jaw goes lax at the accusation. "Face it, Mason. You suck at skeeball."

"Never. I want a rematch."

"Fine. But don't forget you're also down two games to one at the basketball hoop, and the fishing rodeo is my jam." I stifle a giggle, remembering how adorable he looked trying to maneuver the tiny fishing pole with his big hands. And how his tongue would slip out and trail over his top lip when he was concentrating.

"That game is rigged."

"As I recall, I'm up by thirteen fish…and an eel."

"Doesn't matter. I'll catch up." After a pause, a sly grin slides into place, making my heart pick up pace.

"I'm sure you will, my love."

"My love?" he asks, his eyes not wavering from mine.

Heat snaps into the air, and my need for him stifles my ability to breathe. Setting down my mug, I step around the table between us and lower into his lap for the antidote.

"Forever and always," I manage after pressing a kiss to his lips.

"I like the sound of that."

Chapter Twenty

Sydney

Sunday morning comes way too soon. When I roll over in the early morning light, the other side of the bed is cold. While we were talking last night, Will asked if I wanted to be woken up before he left.

I opted out.

I only want to remember the good times and keep them fresh in my mind. Not stain them with uncontrollable tears from impossible goodbyes.

But as I've come to expect, he didn't just walk out. He left behind his heart in another letter.

———

A JOURNEY WORTH TAKING

Dear Sydney,

    I didn't think it was possible, but I fell even more in love with you this weekend. I can't wait to start our lives together like we talked about. A little brick house in the country. Three kids: a boy, a girl, and a flip of the coin. We'll visit the beach as often as you like and go to Ireland.

    My mom will expect us to stop by for Sunday dinner each week so she can play with the kids and give us cooking lessons. She'll worry about us going out to eat too much and want us to have a 'good home-cooked meal.' I'll protest because I cook breakfast every Saturday morning. The kids will want pancakes or waffles with chocolate chips. And they'll get whatever they want because they're perfect.

    By then, we will either be master fudge-makers or have purchased stock in The Richmond Fudge Company because we keep them in the black. See that? Picked up a little lingo from my favorite accountant.

    But no matter where we go or what we're doing, we'll be blissfully happy because we took the risk. We survived the wait. And every second of this journey will be worth it when we're together again.

    I'm going to miss watching you sleep. Hearing your stories. Making you meals and seeing your shock because it actually tastes decent. Every second of every day, you'll be on my mind.

The thought of coming back to you is what will keep me moving forward. Keep me alive.

I love you.
Will

P.S. Speaking of children...what do you think about naming our son William and our daughter Arely? For the children after that, we can come up with something cool to represent the beautiful souls they will have. I can see them and so many moments when I close my eyes — my vivid imagination is both a blessing and a curse. But no matter what I conjure up, my thoughts and my heart always come back to you.

"I'm sorry to bother you," I say when Caroline answers my call.

"You couldn't possibly bother me, dear. How have you been?" she asks and thinking about how to answer had me fighting back tears and longing for Will even more. If that were possible.

"Not great."

"I understand. I miss him, too." Caroline sighs through the phone. "Were you calling for any reason in particular?"

"No. Just needed to hear a friendly voice."

"Well, I'm happy to oblige. Hey, Avery and her parents are coming over tomorrow for game night. Why don't you join us?"

The Jenga game she and Will played crosses her thoughts, and her lips twitch into a grin. "That sounds fun, but I don't know if I'll be very good company."

"You'll be fine, but if you don't feel like playing, at least you'll get to meet Avery and Jonathan can get some hugs out of his system." Caroline laughs. "He doesn't make it weird, does he?"

"Not in the least. And now that you mention it, some Mason hugs sound like the perfect antidote. I'll be there. Thank you, Caroline."

"You're welcome. And like I told you before, you're not in this alone. We're here to commiserate with you anytime."

Sydney knew that, but hearing it still sends a sense of relief and comfort through her. "Now I know where Will gets his protective, considerate nature from. God, I feel so empty without him."

―――

It's hard to keep going about your life when a part of you is missing. When everyone around you is happy, excited for the next day, the next party, the next adventure. The only thing keeping me going is Nora's unwavering support, the occasional text or email from Will, and his loving family.

He sent me flowers at work yesterday, and instead of studying for my finals, I've been staring at them and their bright colors for hours. They lighten an otherwise depressing gray, cold and lifeless afternoon. I have two tests and a paper due tomorrow. It's the last day of classes before winter break, but I can't seem to muster the energy to care about them or the upcoming jolly holiday.

Getting through this semester without Will has been harder than I thought it would be. Like studying, I can't find the energy to eat. Even fudge has lost its sweetness.

My mother's refusing to talk to me. I told her last week after her fourth phone call that I won't be going to church on Christmas morning this year. Even Nora is leaving tonight after her shift at the restaurant to visit her family in West Virginia. I will be alone in all ways possible this holiday season, kept company only by my memories, my fears, and my flowers.

"How's the studying going?" Nora asks, stopping in my doorway and leaning on the frame.

When I answer with a sigh, she follows my blank stare to the blossoms and back. "Have you heard from him today?" she asks, sympathetic.

"No. It's been over a week, and something's not right."

"What do you mean?" She pushes aside the open textbook I haven't bothered to read yet and sits beside me on the bed.

I sigh again, rolling onto my back. "I couldn't sleep last night."

"Why not?"

Unwilling to relive it, I reach under a few loose papers and hand her a small leatherbound notebook.

She runs a hand over the gold-engraved cursive letters on the front. "You want me to read your journal?"

"Only the last entry. The rest is top secret." I muster a side grin and sink into the comforting darkness under the crook of my arm while she reads.

After a few minutes, she sucks in a breath through her teeth before reading a passage from the page. "Visions of him lying in a ditch, bleeding and helpless in a foreign country have begun to torture me. Doesn't help that I can feel him. Feel his pain and fear as though I'm there with him."

Sobs rise into my throat and lodge there as I remember the pain. The sensation of a bullet piercing my skin, muscles, organs. It was incredibly painful. But what hurt more was thinking that it could be Will's pain. What he may have experienced at that same moment.

"You think he's been injured, don't you?"

"I can't know anything for sure. I'm trying to blame it on empathy, fear, longing, overactive imagination, vivid dreams."

"But…" Nora urges, knowing me well enough to expect there's more to unveil.

"It felt too real for any of that. If this deployment continues for years, I won't survive it. And if anything happens to him—"

"Don't even think it," Nora interrupts, but I can't stop myself. It's my biggest fear. My worst nightmare.

"Why couldn't he have a normal job? Like a science teacher or athletic trainer? Why guns and explosives and dangerous enemy territories?"

"He doesn't look like any science teacher I've ever had."

"No, he does not." Somehow, a chuckle breaks through the tears.

"You need to get out of this room. Solitary confinement isn't going to help you stay positive. He doesn't want this for you." Her hand drops to my shoulder, and I force myself to face the light. "How about tacos, chips and salsa, and a frozen margarita?" she asks.

I sit up and wipe my eyes. "That actually sounds amazing."

"Good. We'll go early to my shift, have dinner, and you'll have two margaritas."

"Why two?"

"One for you and one for me. I have to work." She looks at me with her eyes rolling back into her head and her top lip doing an Elvis impression. Her signature *duh* expression.

It usually makes me laugh, but this time, I can only manage a muffled noise that resembles a weary giggle.

"I'll take it," she says and taps my leg. "Get dressed and do something with the nest on your head. I can't be seen with you looking like that. I have a reputation to uphold."

"Thanks a lot."

She winks over her shoulder, and I realize a delicious dinner with my best friend is exactly what I need.

Hopefully.

―――

"Thank you for inviting me over," I say after settling into a stool at the Masons' kitchen counter.

"I couldn't bear the thought of you being alone this Christmas. When I heard you weren't going home, I immediately told Jonathan that you should be with us." Opening the refrigerator, Caroline reaches in and removes the eggs, milk, and butter. "And you know how excited he is to have you here."

"He's so sweet. It's ironic how I feel more at home here than I do at my parents' house."

"I'm sorry to hear that, but I'm glad you came and are willing to get your hands dirty today. Will's cousin Avery usually helps me do all the baking before our big Christmas Eve family dinner, but she's busy packing."

"Is she moving back to Richmond?"

Caroline nods and opens a messy, obviously often-used recipe book. It must have hundreds of hand-written recipe cards, magazine clippings, and printed pages bulging from every side.

"She graduated from physical therapy school at UNC this month and is moving back home," she continues. "It's going to be great to have her close again. She's already lined up her first job. Some big-name therapy office downtown."

"That's great. I can't wait to see the light at the end of the tunnel with my own degree."

"It'll be here before you know it. But don't rush it. The real world will always be there." She hands me a large mixing bowl and a recipe card for banana bread. "Enjoy it while you're young. Before you have babies and a mortgage."

The advice, so different from what I usually hear from my mother, is refreshing. "It's hard to fathom, but Will and I have talked about that." I can't fight a smile when she reacts, her spoon dropping from her hand onto the kitchen countertop. She stares at me. "Too soon?"

"Not for me. I can't wait to have grandbabies." She smiles. "I'm shocked that Will—actually, no I'm not. He's so in love with you, and he's great with kids. I'm not surprised he's already thinking about starting a family. All he needed was the right girl to jump-start it." She smiles down at me, and I blush. "The boy has a heart the size of Texas, and he's going to make a great father."

"Are he and Avery close?" I ask, loving this insight into Will and his family.

"Oh yes. She's like a sister to him," she begins, crossing her arms and leaning a hip against the counter. "His friends were so sweet to never complain about her following them around. She would cheer him on at his football games with signs and face paint. He'd do the same at her dance recitals."

"With face paint?" I ask, picturing Will being rowdy in support of his little cousin at a formal recital.

She nods with a wide smile. "It was the cutest thing ever. They've always been there for each other." She pulls out another recipe card. "During family gatherings, she'd throw the football with him, and he'd play Barbies. We could never separate them."

"I love that."

"Of course, as she got older, Avery had another motivation for wanting to spend time with Will and his friends." Her content grin widens with a wink.

"What's that?" Leaning forward on my elbows, I forget about the ingredients I was compiling in the bowl. Her stories help ease my heartache a little.

"Ever since she started walking, she gravitated toward Jackson." She reaches for the bag of flour and slides it closer. "But as she got older, that gravitational pull erupted into an all-consuming love. Or obsession, depending on how you look at it. I have a feeling she's moving back for the chance to see him more."

"Really? How does Jackson feel about—"

Caroline's cell phone rings as she digs a measuring cup into the flour.

"Want me to get that?" I ask since her hand—and half her forearm—is covered in the white powder.

"Yes, please. Side pocket of my purse over there." She laughs and tilts her head toward a hutch by the back door. "Never fails. Who is it?"

I check the caller ID and rush back to the counter, where Caroline is now mixing the flour with other ingredients in a bowl. "Not sure. Looks like a D.C. number."

"Answer it for me, will ya? Put it on speaker. Hello?" she answers after I press the button and hold the phone closer.

"Is this Mrs. Caroline Mason?" the deep voice on the other end asks.

"Yes. Who is this?"

"I'm Major Tuttle with the U.S. Marine Corps. I'm sorry to inform you that on December 20th, your son's convoy was attacked."

If you enjoyed this Journey Series novella, **please leave a review** on Amazon, Barnes & Noble, BookBub, and/or Goodreads. Reviews are very important to authors, especially new self-published authors since they help us find and connect with new readers.

A Journey Worth Taking is a prequel to The Journey Series. Continue reading the series to see what happens next.

Book 1: A Journey Spared
Book 2: A Journey to Love
Book 3: A Journey Home
Book 4: A Journey Beyond

ATTENTION: Books 1-4 have a different vibe than the novella. Books 1-3 must be read together and in order for the full story and HEA. Potential trigger warnings: Open door (nothing explicit), some coarse language, mention of suicide, PTSD, loss, rape, casual drinking, and violence (nothing graphic). But the focus of the story is Jackson's quest to find inspiration and pay it forward, how he overcomes the odds and never gives up hope. There is more sweetness, perseverance, unbreakable bonds, and unconditional love to balance it all out and tip the scales to a beautiful, memorable, and heartfelt story. Book 4 is a standalone but best read after the rest. Potential trigger warnings: PTSD and flashbacks, loss, some coarse language, open-door (nothing explicit), seeing ghost of a loved one, causal drinking, sick/dying parent, and death of a parent.

Thank you for reading The Journey Series.

About the Author

Since she was a young girl, Alexandra Grace has dreamed of writing a book. She started out with emotional poetry but writing a novel that made readers feel and appreciate was her passion. It wasn't until her 40s that Alexandra fulfilled that dream, and she had so much fun, that her first novel evolved into a series. She likes to combine her appreciation for military service men and women with her heartfelt approach to storytelling. All her novels and short stories are heartwarming, sweet with heat stories that give lovable veteran heroes the happy ever after they deserve.

Alexandra lives in Virginia with her family and is a proud full-time public servant for a local government. She enjoys reading, binge-watching TV action series with her husband, and being her kids' biggest cheerleader.

Now that Jackson and Sydney's stories (books 1-4 & the prequel novella) have been published, she is working on two new bookish projects: 1) Writing a different version of Jackson's trilogy, focusing on his point of view, and 2) branching off from The Journey Series with a new duet featuring Nora and Jordan and new characters Josie and Hayes.

Let's Connect:

Instagram, Threads, TikTok, Facebook: @authoralexandragrace

Goodreads:
www.goodreads.com/author/show/22778704.Alexandra_Grace

BookBub: www.bookbub.com/authors/alexandra-grace

Visit my website & subscribe to my newsletter:
https://authoralexandragrace.carrd.co

Printed in Great Britain
by Amazon